THE BRIDGE

ZORAN ŽIVKOVIĆ

THE BRIDGE

AFTERWORD BY
SLOBODAN VLADUŠIĆ

TRANSLATED FROM THE SERBIAN BY
ALICE COPPLE-TOŠIĆ

PS PUBLISHING 2009

THE BRIDGE
Copyright © 2009 by **Zoran Živković**.

Afterword: *The Bridge* Between Humanism and Posthumanism
Copyright © 2009 by **Slobodan Vladušić**.

Translated from the Serbian by **Alice Copple-Tošić**.

The right of Zoran Živković to be identified as Author of this Work has been asserted by him in accordance with the Copyright, Designs and Patents Act 1988.

Published in May 2009 by PS Publishing Ltd by arrangement with the author. All rights reserved by the author.

FIRST EDITION

ISBN
Unsigned Hardcover: 978-1-905834-32-7
Signed Jacketed Hardcover: 978-1-905834-33-4

This book is a work of fiction. Names, characters, places and incidents either are products of the author's imagination or are used fictitiously. Any resemblance to actual events or locales or persons, living or dead, is entirely coincidental.

Book design by **Luís Rodrigues**.
Set in Minion Pro. Titles in Gill Sans MT.
Printed in Great Britain by the MPG Books Group, Bodmin and King's Lynn on Vancouver Cream Bookwove 80 gsm stock.

PS Publishing Ltd
Grosvenor House
1 New Road
Hornsea, HU18 1PG
England

E-mail: editor@pspublishing.co.uk
Visit our website at **www.pspublishing.co.uk**.

CONTENTS

The Raincoat   5
The Scarf   33
The Sneakers   63

Afterword: *The Bridge* Between Humanism and Posthumanism
   by Slobodan Vladušić   87

*To Ljiljana Pešikan Ljuštanović,
because she understands.*

THE BRIDGE

THE RAINCOAT

I met myself at the entrance to the building where I live. I was just about to go inside after my afternoon walk, when someone pulled the door open from the inside. I stepped back to make room for the person coming out—and stared at my own self.

I recognized myself at once. Not so much by my physical appearance. It's possible to have a double or a twin brother you don't know exists. They might even look more like you than you do yourself. Here, however, the clothes removed all doubt. A double or twin brother would not be wearing my dark green raincoat. It was a recent purchase that I had yet to wear because the days were warm, even though it was already autumn.

The raincoat was singular owing to the fact that its lapels were inconsistent: one was narrow, the other wide. This insignificant flaw was why it had been on sale. No one wanted it, even though it was first class in every other respect. The defect didn't bother me. It was only noticeable if you stared really hard, and I had no reason to expect anyone to give me the once-over.

The recognition had to be mutual, because I looked at me intently for a moment. True, it might not have been quite like standing in front of a mirror, but it would be odd not to recognize yourself on a recently taken photograph, wouldn't it? And that's how I acted—as though a stranger was standing in front of the door. I didn't even nod to myself as a sign of gratitude for standing aside to let me leave, which would have been polite even under these unusual circumstances. I just walked past me and headed down the street.

Bewildered, I stood there for a few moments watching myself walk away and then headed after me. What else could I do? Certainly not go home calmly and pretend that this was nothing out of the ordinary. If for no other reason, I was dying to know where I was going.

I strode along determinedly, like a man on a mission. I was not just out for a stroll. I kept a certain distance from myself, not wanting me to notice I was following, although I didn't look back. I picked up my pace when I turned right at an intersection onto a side street. Reaching the corner, I peered around it. I was still making steady progress. I waited several moments for me to put some distance between us and then turned the corner myself.

We went along like that for around 150 meters and then I stopped and went in somewhere. Since I was about thirty paces behind me, it wasn't immediately clear which shop it was, but I didn't need to get right up close to find out. I am well acquainted with the neighborhood where I live, and I also know myself. I certainly would have no reason to go into shops selling ladies' hats, lawnmowers or pet food. The only place that would interest me in this part of the street was the barbershop. The one I regularly visit.

But what would I be doing at the barbershop? Less than two weeks had passed since I'd had my hair cut, and I always shave at home. What would my barber think when he saw me much earlier than expected? It might lead to a misunderstanding. Spurred by the desire to prevent this, I rushed towards the shop, but stopped dead in my tracks just before I reached the glass door.

I couldn't go in there now. I was already inside. What kind of chaos would ensue if another one of me appeared! It would require an explanation, and what kind of explanation was there to give? The barber might even resort to calling the police to straighten things out, and then there really would be trouble.

I wondered for a moment what to do. I wanted to see what was happening in the barbershop, but couldn't from my position in front of the hat shop. I couldn't just stick out my head from time to time and look through the glass door. Someone inside would notice my peculiar behavior and come out to see what was going on. The best thing would be to go across the street and watch from there.

I found a place next to the trunk of a bushy linden tree whose leaves were already yellow, but soon concluded that I couldn't just stand there and stare at the barbershop. Passers-by would become curious. One might even join me as I watched, convinced that something was about to happen on the other side of the street. People tend to imitate one another. A crowd might form.

I had to be less conspicuous. I went to a nearby newsstand and bought a newspaper in the largest format available. I folded it in two, then tore out part of the inside edge. When I opened it there was a small hole in the middle. I went back to the linden. Now passers-by would find nothing unusual in seeing a shortsighted man with his head stuck in a newspaper, and I had a good view of the barbershop through the hole.

There were no other customers. I saw myself sitting there, and next to me was the barber who'd been cutting my hair for years. He had yet to reach for his comb and scissors. We were talking, and the barber was gesticulating vigorously, which he was not in the habit of doing. He was always reserved. Normally we would merely exchange a word or two about the weather, and here he was waving expansively. I was curious to discover what we were talking about, but even if I'd been a lip reader the distance made it impossible.

The barber finally opened his arms wide, as though abandoning any further discussion, and then moved away for a moment. He came back with a washbasin. He placed it at the back of my neck and I leaned my head backwards. So, that was it. He was going to wash my hair. Well, he'd never washed my hair before, but why get so upset about it? It was nothing unusual. On the other hand, there was really no need to wash my hair. I closed the newspaper for a moment and ran my fingers through my hair. It was still quite clean. I'd washed it the day before yesterday.

When I looked through the hole again, the barber was already at work. He was standing with his back to me, blocking my view of his customer. Judging by the brisk movements, he was scrubbing vigorously. I didn't know how long it took to wash hair in a barbershop. At home I do it in a few minutes. Here, however, it was taking some time.

Some ten minutes later I got tired of looking at the barber's back, so I shifted my focus from the hole to the newspaper itself. On the left-hand side was the city's tabloid news. I started to read the articles, peering every now and then at the barbershop.

What first caught my eye was the story of a woman who had gone into a jewelry store and asked to be shown some diamonds. When they were placed before her, she grabbed a handful, stuffed them into her mouth and patiently swallowed every one in front of the dumbfounded salesmen. She made no attempt to escape. The police took her to the hospital where her stomach was pumped, but this did not return all the precious stones. Three failed to turn up for some inexplicable reason, and not even an x-ray of her innards could locate them.

Then there was an article about a thief who lurked around parks and stole white poodles. He'd already laid his hands on fifty-six dogs, whose fate remained unknown. The police had still found no trace of the man. Even though all the poodles were stolen in broad daylight, no one had noticed the thief, who seemed to be invisible.

The Museum of Modern Art had been targeted once again. Nothing was stolen, but during the night another two paintings had mysteriously changed places. As on the previous occasions, the switch had been announced in a letter to the curator. He'd done everything he could to stop the crank: he'd doubled the guard, set up infrared cameras, and even spent the night in the museum, but nothing helped. In the morning the two paintings were found in each other's places.

One of the headlines reported an unusual suicide on a bridge, but I was unable to read more about it because the rest of the article had been torn out to make the hole. My eyes shifted focus in frustration and I looked through the hole in the newspaper towards the barbershop—and what I saw almost made me faint. I was just coming out of the shop and my hair hadn't been washed but dyed!

No wonder it had taken so long and upset the barber. He clearly had made an heroic effort to dissuade me from this crazy idea. Indeed, how could something like that have crossed my mind? Well, some people dye their hair at my age to hide the gray, but gray doesn't bother me at all and besides there isn't much of it. And what normal person would choose such a bright red color?

I folded the newspaper and dropped it into a nearby trashcan, and then started to follow myself again, this time on the opposite side of the street. There was no danger of losing sight of me: this garish red made me distinctly visible. A multitude of questions swarmed through my head. Above all, why had I dyed my hair? And then, why had I chosen that color? Finally, how had I dared do it on my own whim? Didn't I have a say in the matter?

How was I going to face the barber when the time came for my next haircut? I couldn't appear in the barbershop with my normal hair. Would I have to dye my hair too beforehand at some other place? Furthermore, what if I ran into one of my friends or acquaintances with this red hair? They would be astounded when they saw me, and this would inevitably lead to gossip.

I didn't know where I was heading now, but I hoped I wouldn't stay outside very long. The sooner I went inside, the smaller the chance of an unwanted encounter. I stopped some fifty paces later in front of a wine shop. I took a look at the display window and went in.

This didn't bode well either. I have never drunk wine or strong alcohol. I have a glass of beer only on rare occasions. So what was I looking for in a wine shop? Was I intending to do something irresponsible again? After what had happened in the barbershop, I could expect the unthinkable from me.

I was both relieved and worried when I came out soon after. I was carrying three bottles of red wine in a transparent plastic bag. I hadn't done anything unseemly, but what was I going to do with so much wine? I wasn't going to drink it all by myself, was I? One bottle was enough to put me in the hospital. Had I bought it for someone, perhaps? After some hard thought I couldn't come up with anyone I would give three bottles of wine.

We continued along both sides of the street. Now I was even more fearful that someone would recognize me. I would leave a truly wonderful impression with this horrible dyed hair, obviously set for a binge. Such toying with my reputation was intolerable.

I stopped at the next intersection, waited for the green "walk" sign and then crossed the street. I scurried behind the nearest linden tree and peeked around it. After crossing the street I continued straight ahead. I waited a moment and then went after myself.

Once again I went into a shop I didn't frequent. I'd never liked sports, so I'd never needed sports equipment. I went up to the edge of the large display window and looked inside. There were lots of customers. I caught sight of red hair at the other end of the store, but couldn't see which section I was in because of the crowd.

As I waited impatiently for me to come out, I tried to figure out what might interest me there. My eyes went over the objects in the window. Boxing gloves? No, I shuddered at violence. Hockey stick? I couldn't even stand up on ice skates. Basketball? That didn't go at all with my height. Tennis racquet? Once I'd tried to grasp the rules of tennis, to no avail.

When I finally appeared at the door of the shop, what I was carrying was as foreign to me as everything else I'd seen in the window, although I had a little experience with it. I'd tried to bowl once, but given up after the first throw. I'd thrown the ball with such skill that it rolled diagonally, ending up in the fourth lane to the left.

My hair was no longer the most conspicuous thing about me. Now the bowling ball attracted attention. If they'd wrapped it in the store this might not have happened, but as it was the iridescent red color was painful to the eye. In addition, I was swinging it back and forth by my side, as though just about ready to throw it. People moved out of the way, then turned back to look at me. They either shook their heads reprovingly or snickered.

As I thought feverishly about how to prevent this disgrace, I suddenly halted at a tram stop. Passers-by were still staring at me, but not as much anymore because I'd stopped swinging the bowling ball so crazily. I had no idea where I wanted to take the tram, but it made no difference to me. Just so long as it came as soon as possible and took me away from this crowded street where I'd become a public spectacle.

Luckily, the tram had a second car, so we didn't have to be in the same one. There weren't a lot of passengers and we would have been easy to spot. They would certainly conclude that we were twins, and when you have a twin brother who is clearly crazy, what would be more natural than for them to question your sanity too?

I waited for me to enter the first car then rushed into the second. Overcome with dark forebodings, I went to the front of the second car to keep an eye on myself through the two windows. My fears were unfounded, however. I was no longer acting immoderately. I was sitting on an empty seat and had put the bag with the wine and the bowling ball on the seat in front of me. If you didn't count the hair, I no longer stood out. No one even looked at me.

The stops passed by one after the other, and I sat there calmly in the front car, looking out the window. Finally I could take a little breather in the rear car. I even sat down, although I didn't have a good view of myself that way. I hoped I had come to my senses. We were already quite far from the neighborhood where I live, and this helped put me at ease. If any more foolishness crossed my mind, at least we wouldn't be around anyone I knew.

As soon as I stood up in the front car, I did the same in the rear car. Then another problem arose. No one apart from the two of us intended to get off at the next stop. If I headed back after getting off, we would meet for sure. And then what? I had no answer to that question nor any choice. I couldn't stay on the tram. How would I find myself if I got off at the next stop, without any idea which direction I'd taken?

These quandaries were resolved as soon as we got off the tram. I left the front car and headed forward towards a nearby church. Bewildered, I stayed behind at the stop. I don't go to church at all, let alone equipped with wine and a bowling ball. What was this all about? When I reached the arched door, I shifted the bowling ball to the hand carrying the bag and then pulled down on the enormous handle. I had to push the door with my shoulder to get it open.

I hesitated but a moment, then headed after myself. Even though I didn't feel like going into the church, how could I stay there and wait for me to come out? Who could abide that suspense? I paused before the door, holding onto the handle, and then finally I too pushed with my shoulder to open it. I slipped inside and the door closed behind me.

It was quite dark inside. The only light was produced by two rows of candles on the floor that seemed to outline a long lane from the door to the altar. I walked along that lane towards two people standing at the opposite end. I had to wait a little for my eyes to adjust to the darkness in order to make out the priest and nun. He was short and stout and she was slender and at least a head taller than he.

When I reached them, not a single word was spoken. I shook hands with the priest and bowed to the nun, who returned the bow with a curt movement of the chin, like the top of a pole snapping. I handed her the bag of bottles. She removed one, raised it to the nearest candle and nodded her head.

I gave the bowling ball to the priest, and then both of us headed towards the door. I had to get out of the way quickly because they were coming straight towards me. I looked around and spied some pillars to the left and right. I disappeared behind the one to the right and peeked out cautiously. I was standing with the priest at the beginning of the lane and the nun was at the other end, placing the three bottles between the last two candles. Then she moved aside.

The priest tested the ball in his hand for a moment. Then he bent over and threw it. The church was suddenly filled with thunder. Echoes of the metal ball rolling on the stone floor came out of the darkness from all directions, forcing me to flinch in reflex. All eyes, including mine, were fixed on the glass pins full of wine as the ball bore down on them.

A strike was inevitable. The distance between the bottles seemed too small to let the ball through. But that's just what happened. The priest's feat was much harder than hitting the pins. The ball slipped between the left and center bottle as though guided with the greatest care.

The thud that sounded when the ball hit the base of the altar merged with two piercing sounds. The priest's rumbling shout sounded like wrath tumbling down from the firmament, but what stayed the longest in my ears was the nun's shriek, as though the bowling ball had hit her in a sore spot.

The silence that reigned after the shouts died away did not last long. It was shattered by the sound of the bowling ball once again. The nun had thrown it back towards the door, but gently, so the thunder was more subdued. The ball stopped right at my feet.

I was gripped by fear as I stood behind the pillar and watched myself pick up the ball. Knowing full well the extent of my skill, I feared the damage I could cause somewhere in the dark, far from the altar. The only safe things in the church were the three bottles. I could hit just about anything but what I aimed at.

Sometimes a man can misjudge himself. I was flabbergasted to see the ball head down the center of the lane as though guided by a groove. Sensing the inevitable, the nun raised her hands to her face and covered her eyes.

Broken glass from the three bottles and spilled wine splattered the nun's robe all the way up to her waist. This time there were no accompanying shouts. It seemed to me that she was sobbing quietly, but I might have been mistaken. Nothing happened for a time, as though everything in the church had turned to stone. She was the first to snap out of it. She shook the glass off her robe, then started down the lane towards the bowlers.

I shifted to the other side of the pillar to get a better look. No one had yet said a word. She stopped in front of me and stared down into my eyes. Her gaze didn't budge even when she removed her headdress. Long red hair, the same shade as mine, cascaded from under the black cloth.

She shook her head, loosening her locks slightly, then slid her fingers into the hair at the back of her neck. She rummaged around a while and took out something that had been hidden back there, holding whatever it was hidden tightly in her fist.

I wanted to draw a little nearer, but this, of course, was impossible. I was already standing there, watching up close. When she opened her fist, I didn't look surprised, as though I knew what would be there. Flames from the nearby candles danced in reflection on three jewels.

I didn't take them right away. First I turned towards the priest and extended my hand. He shook it after a brief hesitation. Then I bowed deeply to the nun. The pole now bent almost imperceptibly at the top. Finally, I stuck out the cupped palm of my hand and she poured the brilliant little stones into it.

As I was putting them in my coat pocket, the nun turned swiftly on her heel and headed towards the altar. The priest waited a moment and then followed her, although not as briskly. He stopped at every candle, bent down and extinguished it with his fingers.

I had to pull hard on the door to open it. I went out, leaving me inside to stare at the trail of darkness the priest was leaving behind him. It wasn't until he reached the last pair of candles that I snapped out of it. The nun had disappeared from sight long ago. Unconcerned as to whether someone would hear me, I covered the distance to the door in two steps, gave it a forceful tug, and left the church, too.

I ran after me. I was already on the other side of the street, rushing off somewhere, the raincoat fluttering behind me. From the way I was moving it seemed that I was very familiar with this neighborhood, although I had never been there before. I'd known where the church was, although I had never heard of it. It seemed I knew more than I knew that I knew.

It started to get dark. The streetlights hadn't been turned on yet. There weren't many stores in this part of town and the lighting in the display windows was subdued. There weren't many pedestrians, either. If I were to turn around, I could not fail to see me following me, but I was obviously not interested in what was going on behind my back. We went by a closed tailor's shop, then a shop full of knick-knacks and a shop with old-fashioned chandeliers and table lamps.

When I turned right, disappearing from view, I thought that I had gone into a shop. When I got closer I saw that it was an alley, barely thirty meters long and ending in a brick wall. I got there just in time to see me at the end of the alley as I opened a door on the left and went inside.

I'd made another wrong assumption. It wasn't the entrance to a house but to a shop selling secondhand books. I didn't go right up to it, but I took a sideways glance at the small display window. The glass hadn't been washed in a long time and the books behind it were stacked in disorder. I couldn't get a look at the inside without being seen.

Staying there in the alley was out of the question. When I came out of the bookstore I would run smack into myself. I went back to the street, a short distance away from the turn into the alley, and withdrew into a dark doorway. There was no danger of arousing suspicion since the street was almost empty. All that disturbed the silence was the sound of cars and the rattling tram passing in one direction or the other every few minutes.

Time dragged. What was I doing so long in the secondhand bookstore? I never stayed very long even in tastefully appointed bookstores. Was this some kind of ruse? Maybe I'd noticed that I was following myself and decided to shake me off the trail. Had I exited by some other door? I froze at the thought. I had to find out immediately.

I went back to the secondhand bookstore and stood in front of the window. The dirty glass and poor lighting made it hard to see inside. I had no choice. I reached for the handle, then jumped when a cluster of bells jingled above the door. I stopped in confusion, but no one paid any attention to me.

Although it hadn't seemed so from the outside, the room was rather long. Two elderly ladies were sitting at the counter on the right. They were dressed in identical bright yellow suits that clashed with the dreariness surrounding them, and both of them wore their gray hair in a bun. Staring at the chessboard between them, they didn't even raise their eyes towards me. I went in and closed the door to the sound of more bells.

At first I thought there was no one in the bookshop, but then I detected some movement in the gloom at the other end. I was crouched down next to a pile of books on the floor. Filled with relief, I went up to the long wall on the left. Shelves covered it from floor to ceiling, crammed with old books. As I browsed through them, I made my way towards the end of the room.

Now my back was turned towards me, so I glanced over my right shoulder from time to time to see what I was doing. I had opened a small book and was reading it in spite of the poor light. I stopped about halfway down the wall and I too took out a thick book and started leafing through it. My fingers felt dusty instantaneously.

The next time I glanced over my shoulder, I wasn't crouching anymore. I had stood up and was heading for the front of the store with long strides. I quickly turned towards the shelves so as not to be recognized, and after I slipped by me, I glanced over my left shoulder. I was convinced that I would go up to the counter and pay for the little book in my hand, but this didn't happen. I just passed by the two old ladies who were still engrossed in their game of chess and went outside with a sharp jingling of bells.

I couldn't believe my eyes. I had never stolen anything in all my life, and the last thing I'd steal would be a book. This was a sacrilege! Shame on me! Stealing from these two poor, trusting grannies. I might at least have stolen something with a little value. The slim volume couldn't have cost more than a few bucks. If I'd asked nicely, I might even have gotten it for free.

I could not let me get away with the theft, of course. I returned the dusty book to the shelf in haste, brushed my hands, then went up to the counter, mulling over what would be the best thing to say. It wasn't easy. I'd never had to justify a wrongdoing before. It turned out, however, that no explanation was necessary. Even though I cleared my throat to get their attention, the old ladies kept their eyes riveted to the board.

I stood there before them for a moment, feeling doubly stupid, and then took out my wallet, found a bill that I felt was more than enough compensation for a little used book, and put it on the counter. I stopped briefly in the open door, my ears filled with jingling, and looked towards the counter. The money was still where I'd left it. As far as I was concerned, it could stay there forever, I thought bitterly. No one could consider me a thief anymore, that was what was important.

As I suspected, the alley was empty. I rushed to the end and looked right. I was walking down the street a little ways off, whistling. Matters were going from bad to worse; the thief was rejoicing after pulling off a job successfully. But setting aside the reasons for his satisfaction, who but a vagrant would act like that in a public place? Luckily there were no passers-by. I would surely have caused a scandal.

Whistling all the while, several minutes later I went into a flower shop. It was brightly lit, the only one in the whole neighborhood I supposed, and flowers in large brass containers covered the sidewalk in front of the shop. I quickened my pace. If I intended to repeat my exploit in the secondhand bookstore, this had to be prevented at all costs, even if it meant openly confronting myself.

Standing in front of the display window pretending to look over the flowers on the street, I kept an eye on what was happening inside, although I couldn't hear the conversation. The plump young florist nodded her head, smiling, then asked me something with a look of disbelief, came out from behind the counter and bent down, disappearing from view. When she stood up some time later, she was holding an enormous bouquet of white roses. It must have contained at least fifty flowers.

She trimmed some of the stems with a pair of clippers, wrapped the roses in transparent cellophane and tied a narrow red ribbon around the bottom. The critical moment arrived when she gave me the bouquet. I drew closer to the door. If I took it and tried to run out of the shop without paying, I would prevent this, by force if need be. Even though I had no experience of this kind of confrontation, I imagined I would be able to cope with myself.

Luckily, this wasn't necessary. I took out my wallet and paid for the roses. I even waved my hand dismissively at the change the florist offered me. Her broad smile and bow indicated that I was being generous. I moved quickly away from the entrance, once again pretending to look over the flowers. Who could figure me out now? First I had stolen something almost worthless and right afterwards I turned out to be gallantly open-handed.

I left the flower shop but didn't continue down the street. I went up to the curb and looked left. Not long afterward I raised my hand up high, the one holding the book. A green taxi stopped at the curb. I opened the back door and got in. The taxi driver turned to me, I gave him the address, and he drove on.

I had to act quickly. If I didn't find a taxi soon, everything was lost. I had no idea where I was heading with so many flowers. I looked down the street anxiously but the first taxi that appeared was taken. I felt the cold fingers of panic start to tighten.

Then I saw a lighted sign on one of the other cars. Throwing caution to the wind, I ran almost in front of it, waving both arms. The blue car stopped with a screech. I jumped into the back, pointed straight ahead and blurted out the detective movie cliché:

"Follow that green taxi."

Asking no unnecessary questions, the driver floored the accelerator. The sudden departure pressed me into the seat. We caught up with the green taxi at the third intersection. When we stopped at a red light, there was only one car between us.

The taxi driver clearly had experience in tailing. He avoided the spot right behind the green taxi so we wouldn't be noticed, but he kept the distance between us small so we wouldn't lose it in the traffic that was worsening the further we went. He didn't try to strike up a conversation either. He must have understood I wasn't in the mood.

The trip took a quarter of an hour. When the green taxi stopped, I was filled with bewilderment and discomfort. What was I doing here? I'd never been in the red light district. As I paid, my eyes avoided the taxi driver's. I could only hope he understood that I would never go to a place like this unless I was following someone. I sighed with relief when he drove off without a word.

The flashy hair color, swinging bowling ball and whistling probably would not have singled me out here, but what I was carrying now certainly did. Indeed, who would come to this area with an enormous bouquet of roses? Once again people turned to look as I went by. They even chuckled openly and pointed at my back.

I paid no attention, apparently not bothered in the least. The bouquet soon proved to have a good side too. The flowers seemed to discourage the garishly painted ladies and occasional, equally ostentatious males from approaching me. But I, having no such protection, was besieged.

It was hard to get rid of the vermin. At first I thanked them politely for the services they offered, saying that wasn't the reason I was there. This didn't put them off, however. They started to tug at my sleeve and stick their faces into mine, assailing me with the heavy odor of cheap perfume. In the end I had to use my hands to fight them off, bringing a flood of insults and even threats.

I stopped in front of the only house with no one standing in front of it. It was a low, narrow two-story building that seemed to be trapped between its stocky neighbors. The two windows were covered with pleated burgundy-colored drapes. I smoothed my hair a bit, put the book into my coat pocket and then rang the bell. The door opened right away, but no one was behind it. As soon as I went inside, the door closed behind me.

More trouble. I could stay outside, but curiosity gnawed at me. How could I miss such a chance? I was vaguely aware that the voyeuristic desire to watch myself in a brothel was rather odd, but strangely enough, this didn't bother me very much.

Just a few moments before, I'd felt a great resistance to going in myself. It's always hardest the first time. But since I had just broken the ice, it was easier for me. I went up to the entrance and rang the bell again.

The door opened as before. I hesitated briefly and then went in. After the door closed behind me, seemingly on its own, I was left in reddish gloom. Everything around me was covered with the same drapes I'd seen on the windows: the walls, floor, ceiling. It was as if I'd been enclosed in a box lined with velvet.

Before me was a small vestibule that ended in a steep staircase. As I stood there uncertainly, a very tiny figure appeared at the top of the stairs. At first I thought she was a child, and then I realized that the woman was a midget. She was wearing a long terrycloth robe, also burgundy, and was barefoot. She bowed and crooked her finger, indicating I was to go up.

I started up the stairs against my better judgment. She waited for me to reach her, and then, with a smile, motioned down the hall to her left. I peered in that direction cautiously. The hall was empty, short and dark-red throughout. There was a door in the middle on the right, and beyond it something resembling a small window with the curtain drawn.

She went first, her head turned towards me, a smile glued to her face. When we reached the door, she stretched out her hand, palm up. I stared at it briefly before I understood and quickly reached for my wallet, but didn't know how much to take out. I thought of asking, but that seemed gauche, so I took out a bill and put it in her hand.

Her hand didn't budge and her smile tightened. I promptly took out another bill, which broadened her smile, and received a new bow. Both notes disappeared down her cleavage under the terrycloth robe. She pulled down the handle and drew the door towards her, stepping aside.

A multitude of tiny eyes turned my way, looking at me from all sides except the large empty bed in the middle of the room. I had never seen so many poodles in one place, or for that matter so many dogs of any kind. Their white fur seemed to take on a bloody hue in the subdued dark-red light.

I backed away instinctively, as though confronted by great danger, although not a single poodle made any threatening sound. On the contrary, most of them were wagging their tails. I started to shake my head, horror-stricken. Still smiling, the midget calmly closed the door.

As I leaned against the wall in alarm, my eyes as big as saucers, she took my hand, patted the back of it, and then led the way further down the hall. I went docilely, like an obedient child. At the end of the hall was another steep staircase that we took up to the second floor.

There we were greeted by the same empty hall with the covered window and door. When she pulled me towards it, I refused to go, shaking my head wordlessly. She patted the back of my hand again, and this time stroked my cheek as well. Even so, when we continued she pulled me more than I went of my own free will.

We stopped in front of the small window. Her hand stretched out again. Several long moments passed before I took out my wallet. I chose the smallest bill I had and placed it in her palm, then swiftly put the wallet back in my pocket without giving her a chance to ask for more. When this bill disappeared under her robe, the pint-sized woman opened the curtain on the window.

I didn't look up right away. She had to nudge me in the back before I finally looked through the square glass. In the middle of the otherwise empty room was an ordinary wooden table without any covering. On the right side, sitting on a stool, was a girl dressed in an orange firefighter's suit. Bright red curls flowed from under her high-crowned metal helmet.

She was holding the little book I had stolen in the secondhand bookstore. Although I couldn't hear anything, I could see that she was reading out loud. On the table in front of her was a small pile of torn paper. Soon she finished reading the latest page. She tore it out with a brisk movement and added a new handful of confetti to the pile.

I was sitting across from her, in the raincoat, eating. I would take the crown of a white rose from the bouquet on the table, put it on a plate, cut it in half with a knife, stick it on a fork, dip it into something that looked like sauce or dressing and put it in my mouth. This clearly gave me great pleasure, although it made my stomach turn.

The curtain was suddenly pulled across the window. I looked at the midget questioningly, and she stretched out her hand in reply. I shook my head angrily. She shrugged her shoulders, dropped the smile and motioned towards the stairs. I toyed briefly with the idea of defying her, then gave it up. I had already seen everything there was to see. It would only make me nauseous again. Really, eating roses! I turned and left.

At the bottom of the first staircase I looked behind me. For some reason I thought that the midget would see me out, but there was no one there. As I passed by the door on the first floor, I heard growling and then an angry bark. I quickened my steps and almost ran down the second staircase. As the door opened in front of me, I breathed a sigh of relief.

I was in for a wait. I wasn't going to stay up there until I ate the whole bouquet, was I? In that case they might take me out on an ambulance stretcher. I moved a little away from the entrance and stood by a wall. This soon turned out to be a bad idea. Passers-by started to give me the eye. I didn't understand why I attracted their attention until one came up and openly asked me how much.

I don't know what stunned me the most: the question or the eruption of curses that I poured on the would-be customer. I never dreamed that something like that could come out of my mouth. This was where I was plainly mistaken. Vocabulary of that nature was quite suited to the person currently giving vent to such eccentricities on the second floor.

I felt like going back inside the narrow building and confronting the midget lady once again. I'd pay her as much as she asked, go into that room and sharply order myself to hurry up, regardless of how much I enjoyed what I was doing. Was any pleasure worth the humiliation I was going through?

That's when the door opened again. Not only did I come out, but I was in a terrible rush. Once outside, I didn't stop. I ran in the direction we'd come from, as though being chased, although no one else appeared at the door to the house, which closed immediately.

There was no time to hesitate. I ran after me. The sight of two men on the threshold of old age chasing each other must have looked odd even in this part of town, and the sound of whistles, expletives and even shouts soon started to echo behind us. I wanted the earth to open up and swallow me for the shame.

The chase did have a good side, though. In a twinkling we were out of the red light district and onto a busy street. The catcalls stopped, but people parted before us, sending us reproachful looks. Luckily there were no policemen in the vicinity to stop us and see what was going on, which was the last thing I needed.

Even though, owing to my regular walks, I was in good shape for a man of fifty-six, this demented running was too much for me. Covered with sweat, I soon started to grow short of breath. I would have had an easier time had I known where and why we were running, and particularly how much longer it would take until we got there, but I had no way of knowing.

When we finally stopped, everything seemed clear. A pharmacy, of course! This was exactly what someone who had stuffed himself with white roses needed. We ran inside at close intervals. I almost ran into my own back. The older pharmacist and the young woman who was being served eyed us suspiciously.

Panting, I started to list the medicine I wanted to buy. I listened in bewilderment, standing behind myself in the line. As far as I could tell, none of it had anything to do with indigestion. The pharmacist took three vials of pills from the shelf, each a different color: blue, yellow and brown.

I stuffed them into the pockets of the raincoat, paid the bill and hurried out. The pharmacist was left with her hand stretched forth, holding the change. I felt the need to offer some explanation, but since nothing convincing came to mind, I followed my own lead. Turning around, I too rushed out of the pharmacy.

The pursuit continued, although it slowed down a little. Had I been following someone else, and not myself, I probably would not have been able to keep up the pace, but as it was there was no fear of being left behind.

When we turned off the boulevard onto a side street, the running turned into fast walking. It would have been difficult to run there, anyway, because of the many small restaurants whose tables covered a good part of the sidewalk. I hoped we might sit for a moment in one of them, just long enough to catch our breath, but there clearly was no time to rest.

We did stop in a little while, though. Since I was only a few steps behind me, my loud panting seemed to echo back to me. The window of the store we were standing in front of was full of used theatrical equipment: costumes, overcoats and tricots, boots and ballet slippers, eyeglasses and monocles, wigs, fake beards, moustaches and noses, a jewelry box, a snuff box and powder box, lances, swords and daggers, parts of set designs, framed posters, autographed pictures of actors, programs, opera glasses.

We went in one after the other without opening the door twice. The counter was at the opposite end of the store. I went there, while I stayed by the entrance, staring at an upright suit of armor. I pointed to something on the top of the shelf behind the slim, hunchbacked salesman. The man climbed up a small stepladder and took down two masks: comedy and tragedy—symbols of the theatrical arts. He held them out to me.

I chose the tragedy mask and then beckoned the salesman to draw near. I whispered something to him, and he nodded. I paid and headed for the door. I passed by me without looking at myself, and went out. I was just about to step out too, when the salesman called to me.

"Sir!"

I turned around.

"This is for you." He raised the comedy mask.

I looked at him in surprise, pointing my thumb at myself questioningly.

"Yes, for you." He came out from behind the counter and headed for me.

"Thank you," I said tersely after taking the mask. I doubt I would have known what else to say even if I hadn't been in a hurry. I gave a little nod and went out.

I had already gone pretty far. I had to run again to catch up with me. The mask was light, probably made of aluminum, with slits for the eyes and mouth. It was worn by holding onto a short handle that ended under the chin. The gold paint was scratched in places, as though someone had tried out steel fingernails on the smiling face.

The restaurants and stores thinned out as we continued down the street. They were replaced by low houses in which, judging by the unlighted windows, no one seemed to live. There weren't many streetlights here, and it had already grown dark, so it became harder and harder to see. Even though I was walking close behind me, had I not known that it was me I would soon not be able to recognize myself.

Owing to the poor lighting I couldn't tell where we were when we finally got there. The brick wall we'd followed for the last fifty meters had no distinguishing marks. It could have been a large warehouse or a tall fence. I heard a metallic sound when I knocked on it. I had to stare hard to make out the dark outline of a door in the wall.

A lighted rectangle appeared head-high. I put on the tragedy mask. Darkness reigned once again when the rectangle disappeared, but not for long. The door opened inward with creaking hinges and I was bathed in light. I entered quickly and the door closed noisily behind me. I was alone in the darkness.

I might have been uncertain as to what to do, but the unease I felt decided matters for me. I didn't feel like staying there. I went up to the door and knocked. The metal was rough and cold. A small window opened and a large male head, totally bald, appeared. He glared at me without a word.

As I brought the comedy mask to my face, I wondered whether it might be wiser to stay outside. But there was no time to change my mind. The door opened with another creak and a giant appeared.

He was naked to the waist, wearing only broad cotton pants and slippers. His skin was shining, as though rubbed with oil. He waved me inside. I couldn't refuse that invitation. After all, I couldn't turn my back on myself.

Closing the door behind me, the giant turned and indicated the long hallway extending before me. The floor was covered with a thick black carpet. Framed pictures lined both walls, lighted from the ceiling by the slanting beams of spotlights.

I gave a brief nod to the Goliath and then headed down the hallway. As I followed my distant figure, I glanced at the paintings I passed. They were not ordinary portraits. The faces of the men and women of varying ages were anything but cheerful. They expressed anxiety, worry, fear, even despair. It was as if they had just come face to face with something dreadful. I scurried after myself.

I caught up with me at the place where the hallway widened into an enormous room. It was illuminated by four chandeliers resembling huge Christmas trees. The floor and walls were lined with marble, so white that it sparkled in the bright light. On the right-hand side were six tall windows with black drapes pulled over them.

I headed towards the left-hand side and the massive roulette table in the center of the wall. The croupier at its head was a girl with short red hair and a round face sprinkled with freckles. She was wearing a white blouse and green vest, with a matching green bow tie.

An easel had been set up behind her and a painter was sitting on a tall round chair, holding a palette. He was young as well and sported a thick beard. He was wearing a formal evening suit, and his tie was so colorful that it looked as though he used it to wipe his brush.

On the opposite side was a rather stout middle-aged violinist in a gray evening gown. Her hair was the color of coal and it reached almost to her waist. She was looking at the floor, head bowed.

On the wall above the roulette table hung two large paintings in heavy engraved black frames. The left one depicted a gold mask with its crescent-shaped mouth turned upwards, while the right one had the crescent turned downwards.

When I sat on the only chair at the table, placing the mask in my lap, the painter stood up and set to work. He mixed the paint on the palette a little with his brush, then started to lay it on the canvas with short, brisk movements. At the same time, the violinist raised her instrument and bow and started to play, her head still bowed.

When I too went up to the table, no one paid any attention to me. I stood behind myself, holding the mask behind my back. Although there were no bets on the table, the croupier spun the roulette wheel, then threw the ivory ball in the opposite direction. When it stopped, the long rake used to clear the bets was pointing at number three.

I reached into the pocket of my raincoat and took out the three vials. Without a moment's hesitation I put all three on the space for black numbers. The ball once again went on its circular path. As though uninterested in the outcome of the throw, I looked at the central area with numbers in front of me, arms resting on the edge of the table. I, however, bent over slightly so I could see better.

This time the croupier pointed at number twelve, then reached out with the rake to clear the vials. She drew them in with a skilled movement, without knocking any of them over. They disappeared into a round opening next to the roulette wheel. The rake went up again, waiting for a new bet.

My hand plunged once more into my coat pocket. Again there was no hesitation. I put the three jewels on the space for even numbers. My eyes focused on the table top once more, but I drew closer to the head of the table.

I didn't understand how I could be so indifferent. These weren't pills of no consequence but authentic gems. Where did I acquire the audacity to take such a risk? I had never gambled before. What if an odd number came up?

I stared dully at the tiny ball that came to land in pocket number fifteen. There was a lump in my throat as I watched the shovel at the top of the rake pick up the three precious stones and carry them inexorably towards the opening in the table next to the croupier. They disappeared as though swallowed up by a dark, round maw.

The monster was clearly insatiable because the rake went up once again, inviting new bets. But what was left to bet? The answer appeared straightaway: the mask in my lap went into the space for the first eighteen numbers.

The croupier bowed. The painter placed his palette and brush on the chair and clapped. The violinist raised her head for the first time, and the flicker of a smile crossed her lips. When the ball was rolled for the fourth time, I went right up to the head of the table. My eyes began spinning too, unintentionally following its circular movement.

My eyes kept moving even after the ball stopped, as though wanting to move it from number twenty-six where it had callously landed. Not wanting to watch the rake pull in the new booty, I turned towards myself. I was sitting stock-still, staring blankly, as though this had nothing to do with me.

The croupier cleared her throat. I didn't see what she did with the mask. The opening was too small for it to go inside. The rake pointed to the ceiling again. The painter picked up his palette and brush, but did not go back to painting. The violinist was holding her instrument at the ready, but did not put the bow to the strings.

I got up from the chair. The game was over. I had nothing else to lose. What a dupe I'd made of myself! A man really doesn't know himself, at least not when he's patently losing his self-control.

In utmost disbelief, I watched as I took off the raincoat, rolled it up and put it on the number zero. Although the space was considerably larger than the other numbers, the coat covered it completely, even going a little outside the rectangle.

The painter started laying paint on the canvas in feverish, almost frenzied strokes, as though suddenly overcome by a burst of inspiration. The tempo of the violin, striking up the same moment, lagged not a bit. The croupier threw the ball again, more forcefully than the other times. It spun so fast I thought it would fly out of the wheel.

When it started to slow down a feeling of sadness came over me. I couldn't take this lunacy any longer. I couldn't watch the final circuits of the ball or my own self as I stared at the tabletop. I raised my eyes from the roulette table to the two paintings hanging above it.

And that's when it happened.

The ball hadn't landed yet. Although I noticed the change, at first it seemed a matter of course, like something I see every day. It was not until the large wheel turned silent that I finally figured out that paintings don't change places just like that. The comedy mask should have been on the left-hand side and the tragedy mask on the right. And not the other way around, as they were now.

I stared fixedly at the two large frames, although there was a stir around me. It took a loud noise to snap me out of my fascination. The croupier stood up and broke the rake. The painter angrily jabbed the sharp end of the brush into the canvas, making holes and tears. The violin was on the floor and the violinist was stamping on it in wrath.

The wheel was moving very slowly now, carrying the ball where it rested in the only green pocket—the zero. On top of the raincoat covering this number's space lay the mask with the mouth turned down.

I first took the mask, then the coat, paying no attention to the demonstrations of anger around me. I threw the raincoat over my arm and headed towards the hallway. I didn't linger a moment. I headed after myself.

We weren't walking one behind the other anymore, but side by side. The hallway seemed shorter, as though we were getting to the giant faster than we'd reached the room. He was looming in front of the door, arms crossed on his naked chest. I handed him the tragedy mask I'd just received as my winnings. He took it, but didn't move. I quickly gave him my comedy mask.

The darkness we entered wasn't the least bit forbidding anymore. We weren't in it very long, though. Still walking side by side, we continued down the street, which started to curve to the right. At the end of the bend we reached a new boulevard with a river running along the opposite side. I hadn't been in this part of town, but I knew approximately where we were located.

The boulevard was bathed in neon light and had more cars than pedestrians. We took the first pedestrian crossing to the other side and turned left, going along the river under a row of bushy chestnut trees. We didn't talk. A man only rarely has something to say to himself.

A stone bridge soon appeared before us. It had a low, wide parapet and ornate lighting. We stopped in the middle and stared at the water, where the lights were shimmering in reflection as though in a dark, trembling mirror. A brightly-lit boat full of cheerful music started to emerge festively from under the bridge.

When it had gone downriver, I looked around me. There weren't any vehicles or people on the bridge just then. I laid the raincoat across the parapet, then climbed onto it. For a moment it seemed that I would turn and say something. But I didn't.

I took a step over the edge and disappeared at once, as though sucked in by the darkness below. I didn't watch myself go. I knew I wouldn't see a thing. Just as I didn't hear any splashing sound that might have disturbed the calm evening waters. Leaving the raincoat on the parapet, I headed back to the riverbank. Tomorrow I will buy a new raincoat with lapels of equal width.

THE SCARF

Madam Olga realized she'd made a mistake as soon as she left the shop with a large "Sale" sign spread across its window. The scarf hadn't been expensive, but she didn't need one. She never wore scarves. And even if she did, she definitely wouldn't wear one this color. Yellow didn't suit her, particularly not a shade as bright as this. Moreover, the scarf she'd bought had a defect. One end had two round spots of a distinctly darker shade, resembling the large eyes of a sleeping snake. Owing to their regular shape and symmetrical position they might have appeared a result of design, but a closer look revealed that they were due to a slip-up in dyeing.

Madam Olga, in actual fact, did not like sales. The crowds in the shops and the customers' behaviour got on her nerves. There seemed to be something of the scavenger in their desire to buy things they most often didn't need solely because of the low price. Nonetheless, she was rarely able to resist the call of the showy signs on the windows, although most of the time, once inside, she kept the impulse to buy for the sake of buying at bay. She would usually leave a sale empty-handed and angry at herself for not being of stronger character.

Now she was angrier than ever because she'd not only purchased a defective scarf but had put it on immediately. She was unable to explain this to herself. The frenetic atmosphere in the shop must have been to blame. No one acted normally there. Where had she got the idea she could walk through town wearing such a scarf? Who else dressed so gaudily at her mature stage of life?

The answer to her unspoken question appeared before she had time to remove the yellow snake. In front of the window stood an older woman; she would not have given her a second thought if it weren't for the fact that she was wearing the same scarf. Madam Olga stared at it, trying to see whether it had a defect too, but all at once that ceased to be important. A fleeting glance was all she needed to realize that she knew the woman. Or rather, she used to know her. When she was still among the living.

Madam Vera, Madam Olga's fourth-floor neighbor, had died three and a half months ago. She'd had a weak heart for a long time, and it had finally failed her. They had not been very intimate. They would stop and chat whenever they happened to meet, but did not visit each other. Madam Olga didn't know much about her. Madam Vera was the widow of a retired bank clerk, without children. She'd been devoted to her two cats, taken in by a distant relative after the funeral.

Madam Olga might easily have failed to recognize Madam Vera. She'd cut her hair and changed the color. Before she'd hidden the gray with a black rinse, which suited her quite well, but now she'd chosen red. This might have been flattering too if it weren't for its youthful, flamboyant shade, which did not suit her age. And neither did the scarf, for that matter. But the woman was certainly Madam Vera. The mole on her right cheek removed all doubt.

Madam Vera turned away from Madam Olga and headed down the street. She walked with the short, slow steps of those with a heart condition. She was wearing the dark-gray coat that she usually wore when she went out, even when it was warm. On her it seemed long because she was short.

After watching her walk away for a few moments, Madam Olga started after her, intending to catch up and exchange a few words. Then she thought better of it. She didn't know what to say. She could ask her questions, of course, but was unable to formulate them properly in her head. She might have had an easier time if they'd been closer friends; as it was, everything that crossed her mind seemed like prying. How do you talk to someone who is dead, anyway?

In that case, she would just follow her. She couldn't very well continue on her way as though she hadn't run into Madam Vera. But Madam Olga had no experience of shadowing. How was it done? The street was full of people at this time of the afternoon and she might lose her in the crowd if she lingered too far behind. If she got too close and Madam Vera turned around, she couldn't help but notice her. Then what? And anyway, it was most certainly unseemly to shadow people.

She would try to stay at a moderate distance. Luckily, Madam Vera didn't walk fast, so she would not have to overexert herself. An elderly woman was only really up to shadowing another elderly woman. It didn't even have to be conspicuous. How could the sight of two elderly women walking along at a short distance from each other be suspicious?

Madam Olga stopped dead in her tracks when it dawned on her what made them conspicuous. She took off the scarf, rolled it up and put it in her coat pocket. In fact, she should have done that in the shop, once she'd been unable to stop herself from buying it. It would have been best if Madam Vera had removed hers too, but how could she get this across to her?

Madam Olga stopped once again and pretended to look in a shoe store window when Madam Vera paused in front of a grocery store. There were baskets full of fruit on the sidewalk in front of it. Out of the corner of her eye, she watched as Madam Vera pointed at the bananas. The storekeeper took a large bag, filled it and put it on the scale.

Why does she need so many bananas? she wondered when Madam Vera continued on her way. She remembered the time Madam Vera had told her she didn't like fruit. In addition, considering her heart condition, carrying something that heavy wasn't a good idea. The bag must have weighed at least two kilos, making her lean heavily to her right. If circumstances had been otherwise, Madam Olga would have offered to help, but this was clearly impossible now.

At the next stoplight Madam Vera joined the others who were waiting to cross the street. Madam Olga stood next to a kiosk not far away, all set to cross as soon as Madam Vera put some distance between them.

Just as she was about to cross, a girl handing out leaflets to passers-by, dressed like a majorette in a tall hat and high boots, came up and smilingly offered her a colorful piece of paper. Disconcerted by the rush to make the green light, Madam Olga took it, although she was not in the habit of accepting such offers. She had an aversion to aggressive advertising. She would throw it in the first trashcan she saw.

Not far from the intersection, Madam Vera entered a shop. When Madam Olga reached the edge of the display window, she saw that it was full of tableware. Everything on display looked expensive. The dinner plates, soup plates, dessert plates, cups, saucers and serving bowls were of fine porcelain, decorated with pastoral scenes in pastel colors. Crystal glasses and carafes sparkled in the beams of little spotlights that illuminated the window, even though there was still plenty of daylight. Boxes lined in velvet displayed silver knives, forks and spoons of different shapes, sizes and uses.

What was Madam Vera doing in a place like that? She'd constantly complained about her small pension, saying she barely made ends meet and spent more on the cats than on herself. Had her situation changed? This would be clear soon enough, when she came out.

But this did not happen soon. Madam Vera simply did not emerge from the shop, although she was the only customer in there. This put Madam Olga in a predicament. She couldn't just stand there in the street. She needed something to do instead of staring blankly in front of her. People would start to give her suspicious looks.

That's when she remembered she was still holding the leaflet the majorette had given her. She was certain that whatever it was advertising wouldn't be of the slightest interest, but that didn't matter. She would pretend to be engrossed in something important. Who would know it was just an advertisement, anyway?

The leaflet turned out to be something other than an ordinary advertisement using the characteristic superlatives. It was instead a pitch for a play called "Food". The only odd thing about it was the missing name of the playwright. The theater was in the vicinity and a small map on the back showed how to get there.

When she finally raised her eyes from the leaflet, after reading it several times, Madam Olga stared in amazement at an older man who had just passed by her. He was swinging a red bowling ball as though about to throw it and knock down pedestrians like ninepins. She also noted that his hair was as red as Madam Vera's.

She needn't have worried about attracting attention standing next to a shop window doing nothing. Who would notice her next to an oddball like that? People turned as he went by, staring with bewilderment or derision. If he'd been a young man, such behavior might have been understandable, but it was certainly not to be expected from someone just a few years her junior.

But she had no more time to spend on the man with the bowling ball. Madam Vera finally appeared at the shop door, loaded down. The bag full of bananas was still clutched in her right hand and her left arm was hugging a large box wrapped in shiny paper tied with a purple ribbon. She continued down the street.

Her pace, however, had changed. As though her load were lighter and not heavier, she strode cheerfully, skipping even, like someone expressing joy with their feet. This was not only bad for her heart, if she continued like that people would start to turn and look at her too. She'd known Madam Vera as a reserved, polite woman, but people seemed to change after death.

This time Madam Olga realized where she was following Madam Vera before they reached their destination. She appeared to be sticking to the path marked on the map on the back of the leaflet that was still in Madam Olga's hand. But who went to the theater in the afternoon, inappropriately dressed, loaded down with bags and boxes?

The old-fashioned two-story theater with its yellow brick wall seemed squeezed in between modern buildings with glass facades on either side. Nothing indicated that a show was playing there, but the door leading to the vestibule was open. Madam Olga hesitated several moments before deciding to go in after Madam Vera.

Perhaps the dead could take the liberty of acting indecorously, but she still had etiquette to consider. Although she wasn't dressed properly for the theater, either, it would be even more embarrassing to stand in front of it until Madam Vera came out. She didn't know how long the play lasted. Smoothing her clothes a little and patting her hair, she stepped into the vestibule.

It was full of mirrors and chandeliers, but otherwise empty. While she'd hesitated, Madam Vera must have entered the auditorium. Obviously she had a ticket already, because a curtain was pulled across the ticket window to the right. The only person present was a short, obese middle-aged woman with very short red hair, standing in front of the auditorium entrance. She was wearing a tight, clinging turquoise leotard, a short blue skirt that didn't reach even halfway down her enormous thighs, and military boots. The long thin cigarette holder she clenched tightly in her mouth, even though there wasn't a cigarette in it, only enhanced the grotesque impression she made.

Madam Olga went up to the woman to ask how she might buy a ticket for the show, but before she had managed to say anything, the woman took the leaflet from her hand without a word, pulled aside the dark blue curtain and gestured broadly for her to go in. As she entered, Madam Olga looked at the woman inquisitively, but her face remained expressionless.

As Madam Olga's eyes adjusted to the darkness, she noted that the auditorium was considerably larger than it appeared from the outside. In the middle of the distant, brightly-lit stage was a long table with a high-backed chair on its opposite side. Since there were no actors, she assumed the show had not yet begun.

It was not immediately clear to her why the moderately large audience suddenly started clapping. Then a spotlight hit the middle seat in the front row and she saw Madam Vera stand up and head towards the stage. The spotlight followed her, and the applause did not subside until she was sitting at the table with the box in shiny paper placed in front of her.

Just as Madam Olga was wondering what had happened to the bag of bananas, the spotlight glided back down to the front row and stopped at a small figure sitting there. She couldn't make it out properly standing at the back of the auditorium so she started down the aisle. When she had got more or less halfway, she realized she'd been mistaken.

She dropped into the nearest seat in surprise. That wasn't a child in the front row, as she'd first thought, but a monkey. He had just taken a banana out of the bag on the seat next to him and was starting to peel it. When he brought it to his mouth, a chime sounded on the stage. Madam Olga raised her eyes and saw a silver bell in Madam Vera's hand.

A liveried servant in a bushy gray wig approached the table from the left side of the stage. He untied the purple bow, unwrapped the shiny paper and raised the lid, then started taking tableware out of the box. He placed a porcelain plate, tall glass, silver knife and fork and a pink silk napkin in front of Madam Vera. Then he picked up the packaging and left.

The moment he disappeared, an aged butler appeared on the other side of the stage. He was wearing a dinner jacket with a white vest, white bow tie and white gloves and was carrying a bottle of some green beverage. Dragging his feet, he reached Madam Vera, showed her the label on the bottle and waited for her to nod her head.

He had a rather hard time removing the cork, and then poured a small amount of liquid into the crystal glass. The foam that formed could be seen even from the middle of the auditorium. He waited once again for Madam Vera's approval after tasting it, then poured the glass about three-quarters full. He placed the bottle on the table, bowed, and headed back the way he had come.

Before he disappeared, a double door opened at the bottom of the stage and two men emerged. One was red-skinned, naked to the waist, wearing only brown leather breeches and moccasins. A feather was stuck into his hair, which was pulled back into a topknot, and his face was streaked with war paint. The other was wearing polished armor that glistened in the bright light. His visor was lowered and a sheathed sword hung from his waist; he rattled when he moved.

They were carrying an oval tray between them at least a meter and a half long. It contained an enormous roast bird. Madam Olga first thought it was a swan, but it must have been something larger. An ostrich, perhaps? They stopped in front of the table and placed the tray in the middle. The Indian gave a warcry, hitting his mouth with his hand, while the knight stamped his left foot thunderously on the floor three times.

As they headed back to the door, a tall ballerina in a long, fluttering, orange dress as transparent as a veil passed between them. She started to jump and pirouette, zigzagging towards the table. When she finally landed next to Madam Vera, she bowed deeply. She took something resembling a sword from the tray, cut a huge chunk of meat off the leg and put it on the porcelain plate, covering it completely. Then she seemed to float away.

When the double doors closed behind her, a gong sounded and then faded into the reverberations of an aria. The soprano sang a cappella, as though musical accompaniment would have sullied the crystal clarity of her voice. At the same time, something quite boorish had started: gorging.

You couldn't tell who was faster: Madam Vera wolfing down the roast meat or the monkey gobbling the bananas. Her cheeks puffed up in an instant but this didn't stop her from cramming more meat into her mouth, stopping just a moment to sip a little of the green beverage. Her eyes grew as big as saucers whenever she swallowed the underchewed bites. The monkey soon stopped peeling the bananas. He simply shoved them down his throat along with the peel.

As the feast proceeded, the tempo of the aria sped up and the audience started to clap to the beat, shouting encouragement to the competitors. Madam Olga was the only one unable to get into the spirit of the show. This would not end well. Madam Vera had often complained to her of indigestion. She had had to be very careful about what she ate and particularly how much she ate. Death certainly had not improved the situation. Bolting food in such a manner would soon result in nausea. She didn't know about the monkey, but its stomach would certainly have a hard time with so many bananas, particularly the unpeeled ones.

Just as she was feverishly searching for a way to put an end to this madness, the gong suddenly sounded and stopped the aria at its peak. The brief silence that ensued was interrupted by the monkey's screeching. He was jumping up and down on his front-row seat, tearing apart the empty bag in rage.

Madam Vera stood up. The plate in front of her was empty too. She walked around the table, stood before it and bowed deeply. The audience jumped to their feet and gave her an ovation sprinkled with shouts of "Bravo!" The monkey sank back into its seat dejectedly.

Turning towards the bottom of the stage, Madam Vera signaled with her hand. The door opened and those who'd been part of the show came out in pairs and took their place around the leading actress. First came the liveried waiter and the butler, then the Indian and the knight. The ballerina received the most applause as she graciously jumped over the table and settled at Madam Vera's feet like a sleeping swan.

The curtain started to fall. The applause sped up when it completely hid the stage, and shouts of "Encore!" rose throughout the auditorium. But the curtain did not rise. When the lights came on, the audience sat down. A heavy-set young man in a firefighter's uniform entered through the side door next to the stage. He went up to the monkey, grabbed it around the waist and lifted it with one hand. It offered no resistance and hung there limply. As the young man took it out, whistles sounded from several parts of the audience.

When Madam Vera soon appeared at the same side door, the audience said not a word, as if they didn't recognize the leading actress of a moment before. Now empty-handed, she went along the aisle towards the exit.

As soon as she passed by, Madam Olga turned and started after her. She didn't know why the rest of the audience didn't leave too. Were they waiting for a second act, perhaps? As far as she was concerned, she'd had enough. She'd seen more than she wanted. In any case, she couldn't lose sight of Madam Vera.

When Madam Olga reached the vestibule, the fat woman at the entrance to the auditorium stuck a leaflet in her hand, once again without a word. If there had been time she would have handed it back and explained that she no longer intended to frequent a theater with such a repertory. But since Madam Vera had already gone out into the street, she simply took the leaflet and rushed after her.

How can she even move, let alone so quickly? wondered Madam Olga, doing her best to keep up with Madam Vera who was walking as though her stomach wasn't the least bit bothered by all the meat she'd crammed into it. It must have been at least a kilo and a half. And why had she competed with a monkey? That wasn't at all like her.

They crossed three intersections before Madam Vera finally stopped. Madam Olga felt relieved. She didn't have a heart condition, but she hadn't walked so briskly in a long time. She was quite short of breath and had started to sweat. She was just too old to be shadowing anyone. Hopefully it would soon come to an end.

This time Madam Vera entered a large department store. Madam Olga went in after her without a second thought. Waiting outside was out of the question. She might leave by one of the other entrances. Luckily, the department store was full of people so her shadowing would not be conspicuous.

They took the escalator up to the third floor, where Madam Vera headed to a big section selling musical instruments. Madam Olga stopped at the toy department not far from it. She pretended to look over the little cars, plush bears, toy guns, dolls, puzzles, tricycles, lighted plastic swords and wooden building blocks. The awkwardness of feigning was mitigated by a sudden feeling of tenderness. She hadn't been in a toy store in decades.

Assisted by a saleswoman, Madam Vera was trying out the instruments. How strange, thought Madam Olga. She'd never mentioned an affinity for music, let alone that she played an instrument. She first sat at a drum set and drummed a little. After that she took a violin and drew the bow over the strings several times, then set it down. She raised the cover on the piano keys and played a few notes, but this didn't satisfy her either. She gave up on the double bass before making any sound, realizing it was too big as soon as she took hold of it.

She finally chose an oboe. She held the reed in her mouth for a while, her cheeks puffed out. She seemed to be playing, but there was no sound. She nodded her head in satisfaction and gave it to the saleswoman, then they headed towards the cash register. Madam Olga felt a pang of sadness as she left the toy department.

Taking the bag with the oboe, Madam Vera went up the escalator again. The entire fifth floor was filled with summer and winter sports equipment. It was no accident that Madam Olga went up to the long table with the skis. Until late middle age she'd gone skiing regularly. Glancing over the new models that had become too extravagant for her taste, she kept her eye on Madam Vera.

Of all the departments on this floor Madam Vera chose the last one Madam Olga would have expected. Why did she need a swimsuit? Who else her age still went to the beach or swimming pool? Well, maybe points of reference changed after death. One shouldn't be a slave to one's opinions.

She seemed to have a hard time choosing once again. Madam Vera took a dozen swimsuits in various shapes and colors into the fitting room. When she'd pulled the curtain behind her, two saleswomen exchanged amused looks, shaking their heads. She spent a good fifteen minutes inside. When she finally appeared and indicated the swimsuit she'd chosen, Madam Olga was astounded.

Did she really intend to appear in public wearing that? Why, Madam Olga wouldn't have been seen dead in it. The bikini was not only skimpy but a vulgar shade of red, suitable solely to a young vixen. The fact that Madam Vera was no longer alive was no excuse. It was not a matter of personal opinion. There is simply a line beyond which one does not go, living or dead.

Shopping was over. Carrying two bags, Madam Vera took the escalator down five floors. When they reached the ground floor Madam Olga got disoriented. She'd always had a bad sense of direction. She was convinced that they'd left the store on the same side they'd entered, but they emerged on the opposite side and ended up on a busy boulevard.

As Madam Olga was fearing another forced march, Madam Vera went up to a nearby bus stop. Madam Olga stayed by the department store entrance until the bus arrived. She let two other passengers go in after Madam Vera and then got on too, sitting several seats behind her.

When the bus set off, she suddenly realized she was still holding the leaflet that she'd been given when she left the theater. Just as she was about to put it in her coat pocket until she had a chance to throw it away, she noticed that it was not the same one she'd received from the majorette.

This one also recommended a play, again without the name of the author. Madam Olga shook her head in disbelief when she read the title: "Water". "Food" had seemed harmless too, but that's not how it had turned out. Never trust an advertisement, even when formulated in unassuming terms.

The back of the leaflet had a drawing of the bus route they had just taken, with circles representing stops. One was twice the size of the others, colored blue. Madam Olga raised her eyes dubiously to Madam Vera's back. Was that where they were headed?

Was she intending to take part in the show again? What would be her role this time? Have a water-drinking contest with someone? That would really be insane. But then why would she need a swimsuit, and why the oboe of all things? Madam Olga hadn't the faintest clue, but would soon find out. The stop marked with the large circle was not far away.

They were the only two to get off the bus, which put Madam Olga in a tight spot. If Madam Vera turned around and saw her, the situation would be awkward. She wouldn't know what to say. But Madam Vera took the pedestrian crossing to the other side of the street without looking back.

She went up to the large entrance of a long, gray four-story building, the aperture wide enough for a truck to pass through. On the right side there was a smaller door for people. A tall policewoman was standing in front of the door with a white nightstick under her arm. Red curls poked out from under her small cap. They exchanged a few words and then the policewoman opened the small door and let Madam Vera enter.

What kind of a theater has a police guard in front of it? wondered Madam Olga. Then she noticed something that she'd missed at first glance. All the small windows of the gray building had bars on them. She knew that performances were held outside of theaters, but she'd never heard of one taking place in a prison. Who would want to watch in there? In spite of her rabid curiosity, she definitely would not follow Madam Vera inside the jail. She would wait outside. There couldn't be another exit.

The policewoman gestured with her white nightstick. Madam Olga didn't realize right away that this was directed at her. It wasn't until she repeated the movement more energetically that she turned around and, seeing there was no one else nearby, pointed her thumb at herself questioningly. The tall woman nodded her head and motioned with the nightstick for her to approach.

Madam Olga headed across the street reluctantly. What did this mean? She had never had anything to do with the police. Why was the woman summoning her? Had she committed an offense? Perhaps it was against the law to loiter near a prison. What should she say if asked what she was doing there? She couldn't say she'd come to visit someone because she didn't know anyone who was in prison. And if she said she was shadowing Madam Vera they would probably arrest her on the spot.

But there were no questions. The policewoman took the leaflet in her hand without any comment, then knocked on the small door with her nightstick. It opened at once and the policewoman motioned with her head to go in. The sullen expression on her face tolerated no objections, and the nightstick had started to swing. Knees shaking, Madam Olga entered a prison for the first time in her life and the door closed behind her with a loud click.

The walls and floor of the hallway she entered were covered with ceramic tiles the same gray color as the façade, and the dim lighting only increased the gloomy impression. A large mustachioed prison guard in a dark-blue uniform was waiting for her by the door. He was holding a yellow terrycloth robe for her. She put it on obediently, even though it was at least two sizes too large, then headed down the hallway with the guard. She couldn't muster the courage to turn up the sleeves, which covered her hands completely.

At the end of the hallway they stopped in front of a metal door. The guard took the bundle of keys that he carried on his belt, picked through them, chose the right one and unlocked the door. When he opened it, Madam Olga was struck by warm, humid air, and her ears were filled with cries.

As she was reluctant to enter, the guard pushed her in the back, then went in after her and locked the door. He indicated a brown leather armchair nearby. This time Madam Olga didn't wait for the guard to give her an encouraging push. She hastened to sit down, and he stood behind her, arms crossed on his chest.

An enormous swimming pool stretched before Madam Olga. Along its long left- and right-hand sides rose four levels of metal corridors. These were lined with cells and fronted with wire. Prisoners in striped suits were standing there, banging on the wire, shouting, whistling.

Madam Olga sank deeper into the armchair under the invisible pressure of this noise, covering her ears with her hands. The very same moment she felt a strong pinch on her shoulder. She turned and looked at the guard, who shook his head with a frown. She quickly lowered her hands to her lap and the unbearable sound poured over her once again.

When the double glass doors on the other side of the swimming pool opened, there was deafening applause sprinkled with obscene shouts and screams. A short woman wearing the same yellow terry-cloth robe appeared between two stocky policewomen. Owing to the distance and because her hair was covered by a plastic yellow bathing cap, Madam Olga didn't recognize her at once. She only realized who it was when she saw the oboe by her side.

It's not possible, thought Madam Olga in shock, watching as one of the policewomen reached for the robe. The shouts had grown into frenzied bellowing by the time the old body in the bright red bikini appeared from beneath. Several of the prisoners started to shake the wire wildly while others climbed up it.

Head bowed, Madam Vera approached the edge of the pool. She set up the oboe next to her body. The spectators started to chant something unintelligible, accompanying the rhythm by stamping on the iron floor. When it reached a peak, Madam Vera simply stepped forward as though she had solid ground before her. A hush fell the same moment.

She barely disturbed the water. There was just a brief ripple at the spot where she went under, and then the surface turned calm again. Seconds passed but nothing happened. Madam Olga turned towards the guard anxiously, but he stared impassively ahead. The faces of the prisoners were also turned silently towards the swimming pool.

Sighs of relief came from all around when something started to appear in the middle. Madam Olga had to lean forward in her armchair to get a better look. She didn't recognize the oboe until it was halfway out. But the movement stopped before the whole instrument appeared. The reed stayed underwater, and so did Madam Vera.

Even if Madam Olga had wanted to turn and ask the guard something, in spite of his threatening behavior, it slipped her mind as soon as the music started. She gazed fixedly at the thin silver staff and the wet tones pouring out of it. She didn't need extensive knowledge of music to be enchanted by what she heard. The raging prisoners of a moment before were now listening intently.

The fragile notes of the oboe broke off into the large acoustical space above the swimming pool. As though they were becoming visible, the air started to shimmer with colorful sparkles. The beaming faces behind the wire stared open-mouthed at the quivering interplay. And then the water came to life. Drops from the surface rushed into the air, like rain falling upwards. When they hit the high ceiling, they dispersed silently and turned into watery powder that intensified the tiny sparks of lightning.

The instrument heralded the end of the music when it started to turn in circles. Moving slowly at first, barely noticeably, it turned faster and faster, forcing the water around it to follow suit. When a whirlpool had formed around the oboe, drops ceased pouring upwards and the sparks went out. Soon a funnel formed that became deeper and wider, drawing the silver staff into it. When the tip disappeared into the circular opening, the music stopped.

But the whirlpool continued to spin and the water level in the pool started to fall, baring the rectangular tiles that lined it. The rapture on the spectators' faces eroded into dismay. Alarmed, Madam Olga looked over her shoulder at the guard, but his face was all that remained unchanged.

When all the water had drained out of the pool, a small round opening covered with a metal grate became visible in the middle of the floor. Across it lay the oboe, the two parts of the swimsuit and the bathing cap, but there was no trace of Madam Vera.

Madam Olga stared several moments at the empty hole in front of her and then made a decision. She would stand up and ask the guard for an explanation. People couldn't just disappear like that in a prison, even if they were dead. They must have some human rights too.

But before she had a chance to turn around, commotion in the corridors caught her attention. She raised her eyes and saw the prisoners come off the wire and head for their cells. Their bowed heads and sluggish movements betokened defeat. It was the exact opposite of the sight that had first greeted her.

The cell doors closed one after another with a sharp clang. When the last prisoner had disappeared behind bars, a heavy hand landed on Madam Olga's shoulder once again. She turned around angrily, but before she had managed to say anything, the guard nodded sharply towards the door.

She got up meekly and started after him. He locked the door to the pool behind them and led her down the hallway. They reached the opposite end before she had a chance to formulate what she wanted to ask him.

At first she misinterpreted his extended hand. Did he really expect her to shake hands cordially after all she'd been through? Then she realized what he wanted. She quickly removed the bathrobe, having a bit of trouble with the long sleeves. She handed it to him disdainfully and waited for him to open the small door within the large one. She went out, head held high, into the falling dusk.

Once out in the street she was overcome by a twofold sense of relief. Everyone is happy to get out of prison, and all the more so if there is someone there they didn't expect to see. The tall policewoman was just saying a friendly goodbye to Madam Vera, several steps away from the prison entrance.

As Madam Olga set out after Madam Vera, who was heading down the street, she was suddenly stopped by a barrier in the shape of a nightstick. She looked at the policewoman in bewilderment. Once again no words were exchanged. The policewoman eyed her for several long moments, then reached for her breast pocket, slowly took out a leaflet, and handed it to her. The barrier only went down when Madam Olga took it.

As she quickened her pace to keep up with Madam Vera, she hastened to read the leaflet. She had already experienced enough to know that it was not the same as the one she'd used to enter the prison. She was curious to know what came after "Food" and "Water".

The new show was entitled "Life". Madam Olga smiled. It would be quite fitting for the late Madam Vera to play the starring role. This time there was no recommendatory hype. The front of the leaflet bore only that word and the back differed from the previous ones. When she turned the leaflet over, instead of a map there was just a large number eight.

Madam Vera turned right at the fourth street. When Madam Olga reached it, she saw that it was full of little shops, similar to a bazaar. It was a pedestrian zone and quite lively in the evening hours. There was a hubbub all around, and the lanterns that decorated the middle of the street had just been turned on.

Even if Madam Olga had walked with her eyes closed, she would have known which shops they passed. She was struck by the heavy odor of roast meat turning on a vertical spit, the moldy smell of wet books on a table in front of a secondhand bookstore, the exotic spices wafting out of a shop crammed with colorful little boxes, the sour smell of bird droppings from a multitude of chirping cages.

Madam Vera entered probably the only shop on the street with no smell emanating. Madam Olga looked at the shiny old-fashioned weapons and war trappings in the window. There were swords, spears, halberds, double-headed axes, sabers, spiked clubs, three-pronged spears, crossbows, shields with coats of arms, and banners in various shapes and colors.

The shop was barely wider than a hallway, but it was very long. She saw the lean salesman nodding as he listened to Madam Vera. He went to the back of the room, brought back a thin, rectangular, dark wooden box with a glass lid, and placed it in front of his customer. Madam Olga couldn't tell what was inside.

The customer briefly looked at it and then exchanged a few more words with the salesman as he wrapped the box in brown paper. He bowed to Madam Vera as she took it. Madam Olga did not wait for her to put a little distance between them once she came out. She headed after her straightaway.

They had covered barely fifty meters, one right behind the other, when Madam Vera stopped in front of a man leaning against a wall selling jewelry. Everything he had to offer was in a flat cardboard box at waist height, attached to a leather strap around his neck.

The seller was a short, totally bald man in early middle age. A white cane was attached to the pocket of his long, worn-out army overcoat, and he wore opaque glasses in a round frame. He raised his head a little when Madam Vera started to pick through the cheap pieces of jewelry on display, but didn't say anything.

He remained silent as she took a little paper bag from the pile on the edge of the box. Madam Olga was quite close now and could see what Madam Vera was buying. She chose a wide copper bracelet, a necklace of amber-colored uneven stones, and clunky plastic earrings.

She doesn't intend to wear those, does she? wondered Madam Olga. Regardless of the fact that it was costume jewelry, even if she weren't dead, these pieces certainly would not suit her. She would have to be at least four decades younger to wear them. At her age she would look vulgar.

Madam Vera took a large bill out of her coat pocket and placed it on the box without a word. Her purchase was certainly worth much less. The seller's lips curved suddenly into a smile. He did not reach for the money, however, nor did he return any change. He continued to stand there without moving, staring blindly ahead.

He didn't move until Madam Vera was several steps away and Madam Olga was before him, ready to follow her. He pushed himself away from the wall.

"Madam," he said.

She jumped, even though he said it softly, and looked at him in confusion.

"Just a moment," he continued, as he ran his fingers over the objects in the box. He quickly found what he was looking for. He handed her a small oval brooch in a mock gold frame, with the profile of a girl.

"This is for you."

She had never worn costume jewelry, or brooches. But she would offend him if she refused it. Suddenly she didn't know what to do with the leaflet she was still holding. It made it hard for her to take her wallet out of her coat pocket. But this turned out to be unnecessary.

"It doesn't cost a thing," he said with a new smile, as though seeing her predicament.

She took the brooch, but thought she should make herself clear. She couldn't accept a present from a stranger just like that. But Madam Vera had just disappeared around the next corner.

"Thank you," she replied hastily, returning his smile, then ran after her.

As she turned down the side street, she saw Madam Vera getting into the first of two horse-drawn carriages waiting for tourists. She said something briefly to the driver, who nodded his head and then signaled the horse.

Madam Olga had no choice. She rushed to the second carriage. It was obviously free, though good manners still required that she ask… But there was no time for good manners. She climbed up and sank into the soft seat covered with a plaid blanket.

She leaned forward, uncomfortable at having to order the driver to follow the first carriage. Tourists certainly don't ask such things. What would the man think of her? But before she had a chance to open her mouth, he cracked the whip. The horse whinnied and broke into a trot.

She thought of asking for an explanation, but when she rose up a little in her seat, she saw that the first carriage was not far in front of them. This was for the best, she concluded. The less she had to explain, the less awkward she would feel. The important thing was to head in the right direction.

What she was unable to do, though, was decide what was the right direction. She rarely visited this part of town. In addition, when she sank back into her seat she couldn't see very much. All she could tell was that they had come out onto a boulevard.

They were hugging the right edge of a busy street lined with chestnut trees. Night had fallen in the meantime, and the streetlights created bright islands in the yellowing treetops. Madam Olga rose up from time to time to make sure they were still following the first carriage.

It was not until they rushed through an enormous wrought iron gate with gold-tipped spikes that she knew where they were headed. When they left the asphalt of the boulevard for the stone blocks that lined the paths and roads in the cemetery, the carriage wheels started to make a different sound.

She should have suspected as much. Indeed, where else can the dead end up but in this place? She, however, had no reason to be there. She didn't like cemeteries, particularly not this late in the day. She cleared her throat to attract the driver's attention, but he either didn't hear or was ignoring her.

The further they moved from the entrance the darker it got. When they turned left down a side alley they found themselves in pitch darkness relieved only slightly by the lanterns of the two carriages. Then, some distance in front of them, a place lit up.

She stared in that direction. Was that Madam Vera's burial place? She couldn't tell in the dark. Before they even got there, however, she realized that it wasn't. It was an enormous mausoleum resembling a small house, not an ordinary grave with a small tombstone. It was illuminated by spotlights placed about the ground. The black marble absorbed most of their radiance.

When the first carriage reached the mausoleum it was greeted with a fanfare. At the sound, the carriage with Madam Olga stopped too. Sticking her head out to the side, she saw two figures dressed in tuxedoes and top hats approach the first vehicle. There was something unusual in their appearance, but she couldn't put her finger on it.

They stretched out their hands and helped Madam Vera descend. Then they led her to the mausoleum entrance. The door opened and she quickly disappeared inside. The first carriage went forward and the closer of the two figures signaled the second carriage to approach.

When hands were stretched out to help her too, Madam Olga realized what had seemed strange. The figures in tuxedoes were girls. Their red hair was tucked up under the top hats. They smiled broadly, but this did not reassure the passenger. She would have preferred to order the driver to keep following the first carriage, but she suspected that he would not have obeyed.

She accepted the hands reluctantly. Before she descended, however, one of the girls took her leaflet and looked at the back of it, then nodded to the other girl. As soon as Madam Olga touched ground, the door in front of her started to open. She thought she would go in by herself like Madam Vera, but the girl with the leaflet went in before her.

Just beyond the entrance, steep steps of bare stone led downwards. Torches in iron sconces were placed at regular intervals on both sides. Since there was no railing, Madam Olga held onto the cold, wet wall.

There must have been at least thirty steps. Before reaching the bottom, Madam Olga heard a round of applause from down below. They finally reached a high, round room, lit by a ring of torches at head-height.

To the left of the entrance at the bottom of the stairs was a semicircular viewing stand with six rows of seats placed in steps one above the other, similar to an amphitheater. There was an aisle that cut through the middle, dividing the seats, with three on either side. All the places seemed to be taken. Madam Olga had never seen so many clowns together in one place.

Across from the entrance, a figure dressed in a long purple robe was sitting on a high-backed, throne-like chair. Its face could not be seen because its head was bowed and covered by a purple hood with no eye slits. Gloves of the same purple hid the hands placed on its knees. In front of the figure stood a square glass vessel like a fish tank, half-full of multicolored balls.

Madam Vera was standing on a mound in the middle of the room, her back to the audience. If it weren't for her black blindfold, she would be looking at a large wooden wheel with leather straps by the wall to the right of the entrance. The box she'd bought in the old-fashioned weapons store lay on a little table next to her. Its glass top was raised so Madam Olga could finally see the four long daggers.

The girl in the tuxedo who had brought her down the stairs motioned towards the stand. That's when Madam Olga noticed that it wasn't completely full. The middle place in the second row on the left was empty. She wasn't expected to join the clowns, was she? But there could be no doubt; the seat had a large number eight, the same that was written on the back of her leaflet.

She squeezed in between two clowns. The one on her left gave her a smile stretched literally ear to ear by makeup. The one on her right honked as he blew on a red paper snake that unwound towards her, forcing her to back away. But there was no more time for joking around because the show had just started.

The figure in purple raised its right hand. The crypt fell silent the same moment. The hand plunged among the balls in the aquarium, hunted around a bit, pulled one out, then raised it in the air. It had a sparkling number thirty-six.

The clowns burst into applause and one on the end of the top right-hand row jumped up and ran down the aisle. He handed his leaflet to the girl who gestured towards the wheel.

With her help he climbed up onto two small footrests, leaning his back against the wood, and spread out his arms. When he had taken position, arms and legs spread, the girl tied the wide straps firmly around his ankles and wrists.

Then she went up to Madam Vera and touched her on the shoulder. Madam Vera thrust her hand into her coat pocket. First came the sound of rustling paper, and then she pulled out the copper bracelet. The girl took it to the throne and laid it in the purple lap.

Then she went behind the wheel and it started to turn. It started off slowly, but picked up speed after the first cycle. Not long after, the clown's costume produced a series of dizzying concentric circles on the wood approximating a multicolored target.

When she realized what was about to happen, Madam Olga put her hands over her mouth to suppress a cry. Was Madam Vera really going to do that? she wondered in disbelief. She had always complained of being clumsy, always dropping, breaking or spilling something. And now this, with her eyes blindfolded to boot. Pure insanity. When they die people seem to forget what they used to be like...

Bending over slightly, Madam Vera felt for the box on the table, then took out one of the four daggers. She tested its weight in her hand and took hold of the tip of the blade. When she let it fly, the room fell silent once again.

The dagger flashed and plunged in, but where was not immediately clear. Following the clowns' lead, Madam Olga leaned forward a little as the turning wheel quickly slowed down. When it stopped, the entire audience jumped to their feet with a new round of applause. She was the only one who stayed in her seat, staring speechlessly at the forehead of the crucified clown, where only the handle of the dagger was visible.

The girl came out from behind the wheel and started to remove the straps. But the clown didn't crumple to the ground after she finished untying him. Just as though there were no dagger thrust into his forehead, he made a great arching leap off the footrests. First he bowed to the figure in purple, then to the other clowns who gave him another round of applause. Then, like a two-legged unicorn, he bounded back to his seat.

The silence that held sway was disturbed by new rustling. The girl went up to Madam Vera again and held out her hand. Now she was holding the amber-colored necklace. When it had joined the bracelet in the lap, the purple glove plunged into the aquarium once again. The new ball had a sparkling number thirteen.

Accompanied by applause, a clown from the end of the third row, behind Madam Olga, rushed towards the wheel. She watched in irritation as the girl tightened the straps. She was meant to assume, of course, that this was all just a circus number. What else could it be with so many clowns? While they were all having a great time, she was the only one to be genuinely perturbed.

She wouldn't let them deceive her anymore. She watched impassively as the wheel turned faster and faster, and then the second dagger hit home somewhere. She just waved her hand dismissively when she saw the handle poking out just above the heart. She did not join in the applause that ensued after the second clown jumped off the wheel and bowed to the audience.

After Madam Vera took the plastic earrings out of the bag in her pocket, a third number was drawn: eleven. The clown in the middle seat on the opposite side from Madam Olga ran joyfully towards the wheel. This is losing its originality, she thought. Thank heavens Madam Vera had no more costume jewelry to pay for the throws. One of the daggers would not be used.

This time the blade allegedly hit the middle of his stomach. Receiving a thunderous ovation, the clown returned to his seat, pointing to his dagger as he went like it was some sort of decoration. After the applause died down, nothing happened for several moments. All eyes were turned towards Madam Vera on the mound. Even the figure in purple lifted its covered head.

When Madam Vera started to raise her hands, Madam Olga thought for a moment that she intended to remove the blindfold. Instead of this, however, the blindfold was doubled. The narrow black band was completely covered by the wide yellow scarf. The clowns jumped off their seats and started to cheer. Even the girl in the top hat applauded.

The purple glove stayed in the aquarium longer than before, briskly stirring the balls. They spun all the way up to the brim of the glass vessel, threatening to spill over. But this didn't happen. When the hand finally came out it was holding a dark-red ball with a sparkling number eight.

At first Madam Olga didn't understand why all eyes had turned towards her. When it finally dawned on her that this was her seat number, she started to shake her head. The applause surrounding her was not the least bit encouraging. She raised her hands in front of her as an additional sign of refusal. There might not be any danger from the dagger, but she certainly wasn't going to let them spin her wildly on the wheel. There was no way she could endure that.

When it became clear that she did not intend to stand up, the two clowns on either side of her rose from their seats. They grabbed her under the arms without a word and carried her to the stage. Madam Olga tried to wrest herself free, but they held on firmly. She stopped flailing about when they left the stand, not wanting to give any more occasion for hilarious laughter.

The clowns didn't let go of her while the girl was tying the straps. When she was finally stretched out on the wheel, they returned to their seats. Still smiling, the girl grabbed the brooch from her, even though it was clasped tightly in her fist. She raised it into the air, causing an outburst of delight among the audience. The brooch joined the other pieces of jewelry in the purple lap, and the hood without eye slits slowly bowed.

Madam Olga closed her eyes as the wheel started to turn. She was unable to keep them open; this would make her feel lightheaded and she might even faint. Even without being able to see, the onrush of nausea told her precisely when her head was upside down. But at least the girl had pinned the hem of her skirt and coat to the wood. She didn't dare think what would happen otherwise while her legs were up in the air.

She just wanted to get it over with. The clowns cheered faster and faster, louder and louder. When the dagger finally flew, she didn't hear the whiz, just a dull thud somewhere around her head. The crypt fell silent. She kept her eyes tightly shut a few more moments, then opened them hesitantly.

The first thing she saw was the handle of the dagger above her like a ledge, still vibrating. She thought that it was sticking out of her forehead, like with the first clown, but when she bent her head back as far as the straps allowed, she discovered that the dagger had landed just above the top of her head. The part that had not entered the wood looked ominously sharp.

Then she turned towards the audience. The clowns were sitting with their heads bowed. In spite of their painted smiles, they seemed dejected, as though someone had just died. The girl came out from behind the wheel, her red hair in disarray. She was trying to bite a piece off the top hat's brim.

Madam Vera raised her hands and untied the scarf, then the black blindfold. Her eyes rested briefly on Madam Olga. Then she came down from the mound and went up to the figure in purple. She dropped the scarf and the blindfold into his lap, covering the four pieces of costume jewelry.

The sigh that coursed through the audience merged with a wheezing sound, like a death rattle, that came from under the hood. The purple glove rose tremulously towards the hood, waited briefly after taking hold of the pointed top, then pulled upwards.

When it was plain there was nothing underneath, the clowns broke into painful sobs, and the girl clutched the bitten top hat to her breast and screamed. The headless, empty robe remained upright for a long moment, as though defying the inevitable, then crumpled onto the high-backed chair like a discarded rag.

Madam Vera went up to the wheel and started to untie the straps that bound Madam Olga. She stretched out both hands to help her down. Without her support Madam Olga would certainly have stumbled or even fallen. Her head was still spinning from the turning wheel.

They stood there for a while, looking at each other silently. Finally, Madam Vera let go of her and headed for the exit. Madam Olga started after her without a moment's hesitation. As they climbed up between the torches a chant resembling a rhythmical dirge accompanied them from down below.

The girl who had stayed outside the crypt also held her top hat on her breast, with bite marks on its brim. When the two women appeared at the door, she turned away her tear-stained face, framed by luxuriant red hair. Madam Vera let Madam Olga climb into the carriage that was still there, then got in herself.

They didn't speak a word to each other during the short ride. The clattering of the carriage wheels subsided when they left the cemetery and hit an asphalt road. Lying back in her seat, Madam Olga gazed at the row of chestnut trees dotted with an archipelago of bright islands.

When they turned off the boulevard she wasn't sure where they were. She thought it was a side street, but when the carriage stopped and she got out after Madam Vera, she saw that they were in the middle of a bridge. As soon as she touched the pavement, the carriage moved on. It turned right on the other side and disappeared from view.

Madam Vera went up to the low, broad parapet between two ornate lampposts and stared into the river. Joining her, Madam Olga noted that a dark-green raincoat was lying on the parapet. She stood on the other side of it and looked down too.

The reflection of the lights rippled through the water, creating trembling, fleeting designs on the dark background. A boat festooned with countless colored lights, full of dance music, was coming upriver. They watched it slowly move under the bridge.

When the stern disappeared, Madam Vera held out her hand. Madam Olga needed a few moments to understand what was expected of her. Swiftly reaching into her pocket, she took out the scarf. Madam Vera held it before her briefly, as though inspecting it, then placed it on top of the raincoat.

With an agility not at all characteristic of the elderly, and particularly not of the dead, she climbed onto the parapet. Madam Olga looked left and right anxiously. Luckily, there was no one on the bridge to see this gymnastic feat.

So there was no one but Madam Olga to witness the jump that soon followed. Another eyewitness might have been amazed when there was no splash in the water, but she did not find this at all unusual. Indeed, any sound at all would have been cause for surprise.

She stayed on the bridge a while longer, looking at the scarf on the raincoat. In other circumstances, good manners would not have permitted her to leave one of her belongings lying around here. But the scarf, in actual fact, had not had time to become hers. She had only worn it once, very briefly.

As she walked away, she concluded once again that buying it had been a mistake. Not only because she never wore scarves and yellow didn't suit her. She would have looked quite grotesque with those two large snake eyes. The best thing would be to stay away from sales altogether.

THE SNEAKERS

Miss Anita knew at once that the young man wearing unmatched sneakers, one white and one black, had to be her son. He was coming down the street from the opposite direction, pushing a fuchsia-colored bicycle. Even though he couldn't have failed to see her as he passed by, he kept going as though he hadn't noticed her.

She thought of calling out to him, but then remembered that she didn't know his name. She hadn't chosen one for him yet. Several names for boys appealed to her. She'd narrowed the choice down to three, but was still undecided. This didn't bother her. There was no reason to hurry.

It would be years before her son was born. She wasn't married and had yet to meet the boy's father. She knew nothing about him except what she'd just found out. Her future husband would be a redhead. Her son couldn't have inherited that fiery-coloured hair from her.

If she'd had any inkling that this meeting would come about, she would have chosen a name for him. Now what was she to do? She couldn't catch up with her son and address him in some formal manner, with "Sir", for example. How would that sound? What mother addresses her son with "Sir"? He would certainly be offended, if he was anywhere near as sensitive as she was.

She had no choice. Since she was unable to approach him, she would have to follow him. She couldn't let him wander about town without parental supervision. He might look grown up, one would say he was at least seventeen years old, a full three years older than she was, but he would always be a child to her. She would have to be discreet with her shadowing, however. Children hate to have their parents dogging their steps.

Watching him from a short distance as he walked along, she decided she was quite pleased he was wearing sneakers of different colors. This was a trait he'd inherited from her side. She liked to wear unusual clothes and shoes too.

She was also happy that he had a bicycle. She'd been riding one ever since she was little. As far as she was concerned, though, he didn't have to push it. She'd never thought twice about zigzagging her bicycle through pedestrians on the sidewalk, giving no heed to their disapproval. Even so, it was a good thing he wasn't riding it now because then she would have had a hard time following him.

He proceeded without stopping and didn't turn to look in the store windows. When he finally stopped about ten minutes after their first encounter, a smile crossed Miss Anita's lips. She liked to stop in front of stores selling baby things too. Every once in a while she would go in and browse, even though, of course, the day was nowhere near when she would have any reason to buy something.

She couldn't imagine what interested him there, but this was a chance to find out what he liked. Then she wouldn't have to worry about what to buy when her son was born. She would go into the store after him and see what he bought or at least what attracted his attention if he was just browsing.

Her son's negligence, however, forced her to stay at the entrance to the store. He had simply leaned his bike against the window instead of taking it in with him as she would have done, regardless of the store clerks' complaints. Children can be so irresponsible. He hadn't even tried to secure it; anyone passing by could simply mount it and ride away.

She placed her hand on the large wire basket over the back wheel. This would deter any thief. She looked through the display window, but it was so full she couldn't get a good look inside. She thought briefly of entering the store with the bicycle, but that might be asking for trouble.

She turned her back to the window and stared irately down the street crowded with people in the late afternoon. As always, whenever she was angry everyone in her vicinity was to blame. She started glaring at the strangers coming her way.

Her frowning face didn't soften until she saw a man in late middle age, his hair as fiery red as her son's, whose behavior brought looks of annoyance from the passers-by. Since she herself often received such looks, she felt an immediate affinity with him. What kind of cardinal sin was it, anyway, to swing a bright red bowling ball?

She felt like clapping in support, but didn't have time. Just as she raised her hand from the basket, her son came out of the store. Paying her not the slightest attention, he put a colorful bag in the basket, grabbed the handlebars and started to push the bike again.

This was careless, too, she thought as she headed after him. Why didn't it occur to him that all someone had to do was reach out and take the bag? He wouldn't notice what was happening behind his back. But luckily she was there, not far to the rear, to prevent any theft. What would he do without his mother's protection?

And then it dawned on her that she could take the bag herself! Not to steal it, of course. What mother steals from her son? She'd take it just long enough to peek inside. She was very curious to know what he'd bought. In any case, as his mother she had the right to know.

Just as she put out her hand, he stopped all of a sudden in front of another window. She almost ran into the back wheel. Fancy shoes were on parade in the brightly lit display behind the glass.

She looked at the back of her son's head in bewilderment. She would never buy anything in a store like that. But if he'd made up his mind to be a dandy, so be it. True, such an inclination was hard to imagine given the shoes he was wearing now, but perhaps he, much like herself, was full of contradictions.

This time he entered the store with his bicycle. She hurried in after him, ready to rush to his defense if the salespeople made a fuss. She knew from experience the best way to handle them. She would raise her voice to an hysterical pitch, at which point they would all become accommodating.

But there was no need to interfere. No one took any notice of the bicycle or of what her son had on his feet. It was as though a famous customer had entered the store and could do whatever he pleased. Three salesgirls flocked around him, smiling broadly, ostentatiously obliging. No one paid any attention to her.

The way he made his choice was the exact opposite of his mother. She would have exhausted the salespeople, leisurely trying on at least half the shoes in the store. In the end she most often didn't buy anything and took pleasure in the annoyance she left behind her. All he did was point at the shoes he wanted without even bothering to try them on.

As though the salesgirls already knew his size, they brought out the boxes straightaway. Miss Anita watched in delight as the pile on the counter got higher. She had always dreamed of shopping like this, hang the expense.

In the end there were eleven boxes on the counter. Each was placed in a plastic bag and they were then hooked onto the bicycle handlebars: six on one side, five on the other. There was no payment. My son must have a charge account here, thought his mother proudly. There was a lot of bowing as he left. No one even looked down their nose at her.

They continued down the street. She didn't know where they were going but that made no difference. As far as she was concerned, he could keep walking for a long time to come. The confusion he aroused among the passers-by gave her pleasure, as though she was the one doing something unseemly.

Unlike the people in the street, the doorman at the entrance to the large city library saw nothing unusual in the young man passing by him, pushing a bicycle loaded with bags. He even stood up, raised two fingers to the brim of his beribboned cap, and bowed. She was tickled by the special treatment her son was receiving, but had he taken against it she would have been happy too. She took great pleasure in squabbling with functionaries.

Raising the loaded bicycle to his shoulder with ease, the young man mounted several steps to the elevator at the end of the entrance hall. She was hurt when he closed the door without waiting for her. She too often acted that way towards others, but they were strangers, not her own mother.

She rushed up the stairs, accompanying the metal cage of the elevator as it clattered upwards. Out of breath, she reached the third floor just as the back wheel of the bicycle disappeared behind a door at the end of a short corridor. On it was the inscription: "Old and rare books—no admittance".

This, of course, didn't stop her. The room she entered had a high ceiling but no windows. The walls were covered with bookshelves filled with thick, worn tomes. To the right of the door was a small desk. The woman sitting behind it, her hair graying red, couldn't have been more than forty-five years old. She was absorbed in writing something in a large registry and didn't even glance at Miss Anita when she entered.

In the middle of the room was an enormous white bathtub, its legs in the shape of human feet. Behind the bathtub was a screen with a yellow background painted with many different kinds of footwear, all brown: shoes, boots, army boots, sneakers, wooden-soled scuffs, slippers, clogs. The young man lowered the bicycle to the floor, took the bags off the handlebars and removed the boxes from the bags.

Then he took the shoes out of the boxes and placed them in the bathtub. When the eleventh pair was inside, he grabbed hold of the bicycle and went behind the screen, leaving a mess on the floor behind him.

Noises were heard briefly behind the screen. When he reappeared Miss Anita could not repress a silvery titter. She even applauded in delight. Her son had outdone her. This would never have crossed her mind.

He was wearing only a diaper and the sneakers. The diaper was too small and the tape barely held it up. He had a rubber duck in one hand and a large rattle in the other. He went up to the bathtub and got in among the shoes.

She was proud to notice that the young man was quite handsome half-naked like this. Girls would be wild about him. She would have been attracted too if it weren't for the fact that he was her son. He must have inherited his build from his father. She could barely wait to meet him.

He put the toy duck and rattle on the bottom of the bathtub, then started to scoop up the shoes. He tossed them into the air and watched them fall back into the tub with a gurgling laugh. This entertained him for a while; then he suddenly frowned, grabbed the rattle and shook it fiercely.

The graying woman raised her head for the first time and took the young man in with a glance. Then she picked up the silver bell with a wooden handle standing on a corner of her desk. The fading sound of the rattle was replaced by an equally sharp ringing.

When Miss Anita heard a thudding sound rapidly approaching from the other side of the door, she moved a little away from it. The door opened with a bang. A swarm of children burst in and flocked around the desk. They were barefoot but each of them was carrying a pair of little shoes.

The woman stood up and started handing out coupons with numbers on them from a little blue block. Each child who received a coupon ran up to the bathtub, threw in their shoes, then headed back toward the door, where a terrible jam was created. The surge from outside did not slacken, while the number attempting to leave got bigger and bigger.

The bathtub soon filled up. Before long only the young man's head was visible above the pile of colorful shoes. When a shoe finally slid to the floor, the bell rang out once again. The clamoring around the desk ceased the same moment. Children who had not received a coupon turned around and headed out. No one protested. The bottleneck at the door lasted a bit longer, until they had all left.

The graying woman went back to her notations, and Miss Anita to watching her son. Considerable effort was required for him to extricate the hand holding the toy duck. He placed the duck in front of him, then thrust his hand back into the pile.

The frown on his face indicated he was having trouble locating the rattle. His head slowly disappeared below the surface of the shoes, then went completely under. Miss Anita first thought this was fun, but as the minutes passed and the young man did not emerge, her face grew somber.

She flashed her eyes angrily at the woman at the desk. How could she sit there so calmly while a child was drowning before her very eyes? She wanted to sweep everything off the woman's desk. But there was no time to lose. She had to act quickly.

She reached the bathtub in two bounds and began feverishly throwing the pile of little shoes out of it. As she went deeper and deeper and her son still had not appeared, panic started to get the upper hand. Her nails were already scratching the bottom of the bathtub when the rattle started shaking. But not from where she expected it.

She raised her eyes towards the screen and saw her fully-dressed son as he emerged from behind it. He was pushing the bicycle with one hand and shaking the rattle with the other. She wanted to snap his head off. Was that any way to treat his mother? She might have died of fright, and here he was playing the illusionist. But she would forgive him this time. She liked magic shows. The trick had really been good. He would have to show her how he did it.

The young man placed the rattle on the desk as he went by. He departed without closing the door behind him. Before Miss Anita left the room, she too stopped for a moment next to the graying woman. She picked up the rattle, shook it and slammed it on the desktop. The plastic ball shattered and little silver spheres scattered everywhere. This, however, did not perturb the woman as she calmly made her entries.

At the exit to the library the doorman stood up once again to greet the young man, but his smile disappeared when Miss Anita passed by. He eyed her with a scowl. As though barely waiting for such a provocation, she gave him what she often did to guys she didn't like: she stuck her tongue out at him, all the way until it reached the tip of her chin.

At the first intersection the young man didn't wait for the green light for pedestrians. He crossed the street, paying no attention to the sudden braking and angry honks. Miss Anita joined him without a moment's hesitation. She liked to cross the street like that too. Here was another thing they had in common, although when she gave it some thought, as his mother she should scold him. He was still a child, after all, he might come to harm.

When he entered the first perfume shop on the other side of the street, he left his bike by the window again. This annoyed Miss Anita. He seemed to be telling her he didn't want her to go inside.

As she stood with her hand resting on the bicycle basket, this time she managed a somewhat better look inside the shop. She saw a salesgirl put various boxes and tubes in front of the young man. Unlike in the shoe store, he seemed undecided here. The counter was soon covered with small objects.

If he'd been a woman she would have understood his quandary, but what need was there to pick and choose between men's cosmetics? They were a simple matter. A good quarter of an hour passed, however, before he finally made up his mind. He was already on the way out, carrying a blue bag, when he suddenly went back to the counter as though he'd forgotten something. He spoke to the salesgirl once again, pointing with his thumb behind his back, towards the window.

Miss Anita was puzzled. Was he pointing at her? She felt like hightailing it the same instant, but she couldn't leave the bike. It isn't easy with children, she concluded. They put you in impossible positions. As she was pondering what to do, the salesgirl went up to the window and took a long red wig off one of the gray plastic busts.

What does he need that for? wondered Miss Anita, caught in a dilemma. She brightened at the thought that he might be buying it for her. How nice! He wants his mother to have hair like his. She had never worn a wig, and up until then red had never been her favorite color, but she would certainly accept the gift. How could she refuse it?

But no gift was presented to her when the young man left the perfume shop. Once again he took absolutely no notice of her standing by the bicycle. He just put the blue bag in the basket and continued down the street. Offended, she stared at his back for several moments, then headed after him. If it had been anyone else, she would have made a scene. But her son, of course, was an exception.

The next time he stopped was in front of another luxury boutique. As she watched him enter, pushing the bicycle, she wondered in confusion what he was doing in a fancy shop selling women's lingerie.

Had she been on her own, she would never have set foot in there, but now it was clear she had to go in after him. She went quite unnoticed here too. Both salesgirls devoted their attention solely to the young man. There was no need to say anything. As though knowing what he'd come for, they hastened to a marble shelf and took down a thin box with a large gold crown embossed on it.

Miss Anita didn't wear such lingerie; moreover, she despised it. Even so, the pink silk camisole with thin straps and lace trim that was taken out of the box filled her with admiration. She tried to imagine herself in it. Suddenly there was nothing objectionable about it.

The young man just nodded briefly. The camisole was folded and returned to the box, which was wrapped in turquoise paper and tied with a dark blue ribbon. There was no payment this time either. With another nod, the customer took the box, put it under his arm and went out.

On a square not far from the shop, the young man halted at a trolleybus stop. Miss Anita smiled. Bicycles were not allowed in trolleybuses, but she still took hers in from time to time. Once she'd caused a traffic jam because the driver refused to continue until she got off. She did in the end, but only after someone had called the police.

When they entered the trolleybus, there was none of the usual grumbling from the other passengers. On the contrary, they were kind enough to make room for the bike at the back of the bus. This exasperated Miss Anita to no end. How unfair! Had she been the one, she would have already received a torrent of disapproval and even insults, while here they were all looking kindly on her son. Although she was aware that this should actually please her, she felt a pang of jealousy.

After they had passed several stops, a much stronger wave of jealousy washed over her. Why hadn't she thought of it before? Of course! Everything he'd bought in the perfumery and lingerie shop had been not for her, as she'd naively thought, but for some other woman. She barely suppressed the impulse to go up and give him a resounding slap in front of everyone.

Oh well, she must reconcile herself to the fact that one day he would leave her for someone else, he couldn't stay with his mother forever. But it wasn't time for that yet, why, she'd only just met him. Perhaps she was berating him unjustly. He couldn't be the one to blame, of course, he was too young and inexperienced.

Someone must have turned his head. The type wasn't hard to imagine. Certainly an older and unattractive woman. They liked to pounce on young men. But rich too. Of course! That's why he had charge accounts in fancy shops.

Wonderful. Since he was clearly heading for a rendezvous with her, this was a chance to tell the old bag what she thought about this seduction of her son. Buying him, actually. When she got her hands on the woman feathers would fly.

But when they got off the trolleybus she saw they were not in the part of town with villas surrounded by tall hedges, as she'd supposed. The neighborhood was rather gloomy. Gray four-story buildings lined both sides of the street and there were no shops.

They went some fifty meters and then he stopped in front of a house without a single window. The only thing interrupting the uniform olive-green façade was a small black door. Next to it was a dusty brass plate with the inscription: "City Mental Institution".

She did not enter immediately after her son. A rare feeling of guilt oppressed her. Accepting any woman he was attached to, old floozy or not, would be hard. But if he'd set his heart on someone from this place, that was another matter altogether. She felt kindly towards the poor souls locked up in there. People often said that she too was crazy just because she was unconventional.

She thought she'd find a guard behind the door, but no one was there when she entered. At the end of a long corridor she saw her son lean the bike against a wall, take the blue bag out of the basket and disappear off somewhere to the right. When she got there, she found stairs winding downwards.

Having descended after him, she found herself at the beginning of a new corridor, considerably shorter than the one above. There was a metal door to the left of the stairs and another with a reinforced glass window at the end of the corridor, which the young man had just closed behind him. When she got up close enough she managed to read the tiny inscription on the plate under the window: "Kitchen".

She pressed down on the handle, but the door didn't open. She tried once again, pushing with her shoulder, again with no result. Angered, she put her face against the window and looked inside.

A large table filled the middle of the room, while the walls were lined with shelves, cabinets, refrigerators and ovens. To either side of the table were three men wearing light-green pants, sleeveless undershirts and toques. They were rolling out dough with wide rolling pins and it covered almost the whole surface of the table.

Miss Anita put her face right up against the window so she could see the perimeter of the room, but her son was nowhere to be seen. He must have gone through the door on the right that probably led to the pantry. But why was he in there? Or rather, what on earth was he doing in the kitchen? Was he intending to treat his chosen one with something sweet? That would be nice. She liked to receive sweets, too.

Minutes passed and nothing happened. The cooks rolled their pins over the dough with harmonious movements, as though to a rhythm of music that couldn't be heard in the corridor. Miss Anita couldn't imagine what enormous thing they were preparing.

Finally they raised their rolling pins and looked towards the side door. Again she pressed her cheek against the metal edge of the window. A girl with long red hair stepped out of the pantry into the kitchen. She was wearing nothing but the pink camisole and was garishly made up in matching shades.

So that's it, thought Miss Anita. This is where they have their secret rendezvous. Clever. She couldn't see very well at such an angle through the reinforced glass, but the girl seemed attractive. She was almost as tall as her son, with regular facial features that seemed somehow familiar.

Head bowed, clearly feeling awkward, the girl headed around the table. When she was standing next to the cook in the middle, she started to go down and quickly disappeared from Miss Anita's sight. Her first thought was that the girl had gone down through an opening in the floor, which must certainly be the beginning of a secret passage taking her back to her cell without being seen.

But then the three cooks from that side of the table disappeared as well. What did this mean? And where was her son? Why hadn't he come out of the pantry? Nothing happened for a few moments, and then four figures came up from behind the table.

The three cooks had raised the girl horizontally, holding her under the shoulders, hips and calves. Even before Miss Anita caught sight of the black and white sneakers, she understood her initial misconception. Her eyes grew as round as saucers.

There had been no older woman or girl. What he'd bought in the last two stores was for him: the cosmetics, wig and camisole. She'd never imagined in her wildest dreams that her son would have such inclinations. How horrible! What was she to do? What position should she take? She couldn't forsake him, could she? She would have to accept him as he was. She was his mother, after all. How could she turn her back on him?

But that wasn't the most important thing at the moment. What did these strapping men want from him? Why, he was still a child, so to speak. She watched in bewilderment as they carried her son's rigid body to the middle of the table. Putting aside their rolling pins, three new pairs of hands stretched out from the other side and held him under the back and feet.

He lay there briefly without moving, as though in a living net, and then the hands started to descend. They slipped out deftly right above the tabletop, lowering the young man into the middle of the dough. What did these perverts have in mind? Although still willing to accept the fact that her son wasn't normal, she wasn't about to watch any debauchery.

But what she vaguely anticipated did not happen. The cooks started to slip their fingers under the dough along the edge of the table. When their hands reached the young man's body, they wrapped first one side of the sheet-like shroud over him and then the other.

Now he was lying in the middle of the table rolled up like an enormous sausage roll, his unmatched sneakers sticking out of one end and his tuft of red hair from the other. He'll suffocate inside, thought his mother frantically. Are these monsters at all aware of the fact?

And then she discovered there are worse fates than suffocation. One of the cooks approached the left-hand wall. She noted with alarm that the rectangular door belonged to a large oven and not a white cabinet. The cook opened it, then stepped back from the intense heat.

Fused to the small window, Miss Anita watched in disbelief as the six cooks picked up what she'd thought was the tabletop, but was actually a large tin surface. The end with the red wig sticking out soon started to enter the glowing hot compartment.

Miss Anita banged her fists on the window hysterically and started to scream. But no one in the kitchen paid any attention. The baking tin with her son wrapped in dough was steadily disappearing into the oven. When the sneakers were inside too, they closed the door.

Their job finished, the six cooks headed for the other side of the kitchen. One by one they entered the room which the young man disguised as a girl had left just a few minutes before.

Completely beside herself, Miss Anita started to kick the door and tug at the handle. The small corridor was now echoing with noise. If there was no one here in the basement, she reasoned, finally managing a coherent thought, there must be someone upstairs. This was indeed a madhouse, but not all of them had to be crazy.

Just as she turned to go up, the door next to the stairs opened. She stopped in mid-step and stared at her son standing in the doorway. He looked quite normal, as though the travesties of a moment before, wrapping him in sticky dough and putting him in the oven, had been inflicted on someone else entirely. He ran up the steps.

Miss Anita saw red. Her helplessness and despair were instantly transformed into the quintessence of rage. Now he was in for it. Once she was through with him, he would never think of practicing his stupid circus tricks on her again. She could have died of panic. She hastened after him.

When she reached the top of the stairs, he was just going out of the black door into the street. As soon as she emerged into the falling dusk, she realized it wouldn't be easy to get her hands on him. He was pedaling fast and furiously on the bike, disappearing down the street. She stamped her feet on the pavement in frustration, then headed off in hot pursuit.

She paid no attention to the occasional passers-by who scrambled out of her way. She only growled at one of them who made a remark. It wasn't until they'd traveled three blocks that she realized her son wasn't trying to get away from her. Had he wanted to, he could have easily gone beyond her reach. His cycling speed was just enough to maintain the distance between them. When she started to pant and slow down, he did the same.

Exhaustion eased the rage that had consumed her. She was still mad at him for playing with her so cold-heartedly in the basement of the insane asylum, but now what annoyed her was the fact that she had no way of knowing when this dashing about would end. It wasn't fair for him to be on a bicycle while she jogged along.

She quickened her pace when he turned a corner. What she found when she got there was a side street with an open-air flea market. Both sides of the street were lined with stalls, some covered, some not, and the pavement in between was filled with people. Her son was off the bike and had just joined the throng. She picked up her pace so as not to lose sight of him.

He wandered from stall to stall, browsing idly. Even if he'd wanted to walk faster, he couldn't because of the bicycle. A wide variety of used goods were on sale, arranged without rhyme or reason: vases, candlesticks, shabby hats, gilded buttons, cracked cigarette holders, garden gloves, inkpots, castanets, paper cutters, corkscrews, phonograph records without jackets, nail clippers, monocle frames, dolls' clothes, bundles of letters, wooden legs, porcelain chamber pots, old-fashioned radios, rusty hair clippers, harmonicas, monogrammed napkins, batteries, shoe inserts, dental forceps, salt shakers.

She couldn't resist the temptation for long. She didn't need any of those old things, but she never stole because she was in need. It was just for the thrill of it. She never kept the things she stole and always left them where their appearance would cause confusion, as she watched surreptitiously and laughed.

They worked like a well-drilled team. He would cause a disturbance as he maneuvered his bicycle to get close to a stall, and she would take advantage of this distraction to steal something. Her fingers were swift and skillful. Even if someone was watching they would have a hard time noticing anything. Because of the help he was inadvertently giving her, she had already forgiven her son what he'd done to her in the madhouse.

First she stole a rather large eight-branched medal with a blue and white ribbon. She almost cried out when she pricked herself on one of the sharp points. Then she took something wrapped in paper. She unwrapped it in her coat pocket, and when she touched the object her faced twisted in disgust. She removed the false teeth, holding them gingerly with two fingers, placed them on the ground next to her foot and crushed them in anger. She shot the seller a piercing look.

She was almost caught in the act when she picked a white pipe off an overcrowded stall. When she pulled it out, the small pile of objects resting on it collapsed. But this didn't attract the seller's attention and he didn't interrupt his conversation with a customer at the other end of the stall. The pipe soon joined the medal in Miss Anita's pocket.

Another item ended up on the ground. She thought that the pink dice with white spots denoting numbers one to six was made of marble, but when she found out it was plastic, she threw it away in disgust. This seller received a dark look too. How did they have the nerve to sell such junk?

The last little thing she stole was the least valuable, but she liked it the most. As a little girl she'd had something similar, but hadn't seen one for sale in a long time. Inside the tiny glass snow globe was a house surrounded by a garden in some kind of liquid.

She knew what would happen if she shook the globe. Snow would start to fall on the house. As a little girl she would stare at length at the particles falling slowly on Santa's sleigh. She wanted to see that again, but would have to move at least a short distance away from the stall. She put her hand in her pocket but didn't let go of the snow globe for fear that the medal's spikes would damage it.

She decided to keep it. She would drop the other two items on the next stall, but not the snow globe. This would be her first real theft, although for some reason her conscience wasn't bothered. The seller probably didn't even know he had it in his pile of trinkets.

Nonetheless, as they continued on their way, he spoke to her. "There will be lots of snow this winter, young lady." She turned around and looked apprehensively at the short, heavy-set man behind the stall, who was smiling. He was wearing a tasseled orange knit cap. Before she had a chance to reply, he turned to another customer.

The crowd thinned briefly. They were at an intersection that interrupted the two rows of stalls. The flea market continued straight ahead, and a narrow little street went off left and right, its poor lighting emphasized by the deepening night. The young man pushed his bike to the left. As she followed him, she thought for a moment of simply dumping the medal and pipe, but then felt this would be out of place.

The hubbub subsided the farther they got from the flea market. There had been a few people at the beginning of the backstreet, but now they hadn't encountered anyone for some time. In addition, fewer and fewer of the store and house windows were lit. The low, dilapidated houses of sooty brick that now surrounded them seemed abandoned.

She finally decided to ask him where they were headed. As a mother she had a right to know. But then he stopped before a door that looked just the same as the others. He leaned the bicycle against the wall and knocked three times. No one responded, or at least not that she heard. He, however, concluded after a short wait that he could enter. He left the door ajar.

She hesitated just a moment before entering. If he thought his bicycle was safe there outside, so be it. She had no intention of standing guard anymore. He was gravely mistaken if he expected her to do such things without letup. She was his mother, not his nursemaid.

She found herself in a long and narrow corridor. Somewhere in the distance a bulb with a round metal shade was swinging on a cord, even though there was no draft. The young man was outlined in the dim light. She rushed to catch up with him.

At the end of the corridor were steps leading down. They descended into a small room, also dimly lit. Another shaded light bulb was swinging back and forth. The place smelled of wet coal, although there was nothing but shelves full of empty, dusty bottles and jars along the left-hand wall.

Another door on the opposite wall opened onto a staircase leading up. They ascended cautiously because of the dark. The only light came from somewhere way up high. The wooden steps creaked under their feet as they climbed, holding onto the wobbly handrail.

If she remembered correctly, none of the buildings on the street was more than two floors high. Here, however, they climbed up all of five floors before they reached a small round room at the top bathed in light. Three tin mushroom-lights with short shiny stalks swung in harmony from the ceiling, forming a moving equilateral triangle.

The round table in the middle of the room had a single fat leg firmly fixed to the floor. Two domes of the same wood, resembling humps, rose from the tabletop.

Behind the table was a large barrel. The man standing in it was naked from the waist up, his shoulders, arms and head shiny as though rubbed with oil. The feminine features of his round face were emphasized by the thick braid of bushy red hair that sprouted at the back of his head and disappeared into the barrel.

When the visitors appeared at the door to the little room he gave a resounding clap. The three bright lights suddenly started swinging faster. He pointed at the humps with his right hand as his lips curved into a seductive smile.

The young man went up to the table, then turned towards Miss Anita who had stayed at the entrance. They looked at each other briefly, without a word, and then she headed towards him with slow steps.

When she was standing next to him, he raised his hand in front of her, palm up. She stared at it with a frown, and several long moments passed before she began rummaging through her coat pocket.

She took out the sharp-pointed medal with care and placed it in her son's hand. But the hand didn't move. She gave him a long, piercing look, her lips pursed in an angry grimace, before she reached into her pocket once again. The pipe was placed next to the medal in his hand.

The hand, however, was still waiting. Miss Anita started to shake her head. The anger on her face dissolved into a contorted plea. But he was unrelenting. The tips of his fingers even curled several times impatiently, hurrying her up. With glistening eyes she lowered the snow globe into the insatiable hand, but there were no tears.

The three objects quickly passed from one hand into another. The braided head bowed and his smile broadened. His hand disappeared into the barrel for a moment and laid the medal, pipe and snow globe down there.

When his hand re-emerged, he grabbed hold of the round table and gave it a sharp spin. The speed of its rotation transformed the two domes into the illusion of a single peak in the middle of the tabletop. The effect was soon destroyed as it began to slow down. Finally, the table was stationary once again.

Two plump hands with short fingers, palms up, motioned towards the two domes as though they had something to offer. The young man didn't hesitate a moment. He indicated the one on his right.

With a new bow, the man in the barrel took hold of the brass handle on the top of the dome and picked it up. Protracted giggling filled the little room when there was nothing underneath it. That same moment one of the three lights flickered and went out.

The young man looked at Miss Anita. There was no regret in his eyes. Just as hers had a moment before, his lips pursed in anger. The look she returned was a mixture of reproof and compassion.

He dropped down on his left knee and started to untie the lace on his right, white sneaker. His movements were nervous. He pulled the shoe off his foot half unlaced, stood up and offered it to the bare torso.

He was rewarded with another smile and bow as this wager also disappeared into the barrel. The Bactrian camel briefly became a dromedary and then returned to its initial shape.

The choice this time was preceded by hesitation. The young man's hand hovered between the two domes, and then he finally pointed his index finger at the right hand one again. This time the giggle seemed to echo from the emptiness underneath it. There was even soft feminine applause as the second light went out. The lighting in the little room was now as dim as in the basement.

The young man started to turn towards Miss Anita, but then changed his mind. He suddenly raised his left foot and yanked off the black sneaker without undoing the laces. The barrel's maw swallowed the third wager.

The table seemed to spin forever. When it finally stopped, no one moved for a moment. This standstill was shattered by the young man, but not in order to choose a dome. Moving swiftly, he grabbed both handles and pulled them up.

That same moment, the bare-chested man closed his eyes and started to sing as he sank into the barrel. The soprano carved a crystal dirge in the air that changed its timbre when the head sank out of sight. Once it was gone, the two extinguished lights turned back on, illuminating the little room once again. None of the three lights was swinging anymore.

Miss Anita watched wordlessly as the young man placed the wooden domes on the floor and took the black and white sneakers from the table. He patiently loosened the laces and then put them on. When he was finished tying the bows, the voice in the barrel fell silent.

There was a groan from inside, then the cut-off braid flew out and landed on the empty table. Miss Anita reflected that many years were needed to grow hair long enough for a braid like that.

When the young man grabbed her hand she tried to pull it free, but his grip was firm. He led her out of the little room. Although the stairs were shaky, they ran down all five flights, not bothering to hold onto the rail.

They sped through the basement room with several strides. She had just enough time to notice that the light had stopped swinging there too. The other change, however, was considerably more pronounced. Not a single one of the bottles and jars seemed to be intact. Slivers of broken glass covered the floor under the shelves now fronting the right-hand wall.

The light in the long corridor was barely flickering. If the young man hadn't been leading her, she would have had to advance with caution. They did not go out of the door as soon as they reached it. He knocked three times as before, and then waited. Once again she didn't hear anything before he finally opened the door and led her outside.

She breathed a sigh of relief when she saw the bicycle waiting for them. The thought that her son had a lucky streak brought a smile to her lips. But her smile disappeared when she saw him jump on the bike. He was gravely mistaken if he thought she was about to rush after him again.

He didn't leave without her, however. He nodded his head at the fuchsia-colored bar that joined the seat to the handlebars. She looked at him quizzically for a moment, then sat down and grabbed hold of the inner sides of the handlebars. It was a little uncomfortable, but certainly better than running.

They reached the flea market in no time at all. Night had already fallen so there weren't many people and they could continue without stopping. They did have to ring the bell, though.

Miss Anita's initial anxiety was replaced by delight. She greatly enjoyed watching people jump aside to let the bicycle pass. This was often accompanied by scolding and curses. Several times she turned around and made faces at them.

They picked up speed dangerously when they left the flea market. There was more honking and screeching of brakes as they coasted down the middle of the street. Miss Anita screamed in reply and thrashed her legs dangling down the sides.

She didn't know where they were headed, but that made no difference. She was safe in the hands of her son and nothing bad could happen to her. She hadn't had such a good time in ages.

They soon came out onto a boulevard lined with chestnut trees. The embanked side of a river stretched along one side. The young man turned off the pavement onto the sidewalk, under bushy treetops. Too bad there are so few people on the promenade, thought Miss Anita. It would look much more cheerful.

When they reached a stone bridge, the young man stopped the bicycle. He waited for her to get down and then got off too. He climbed up onto a wide parapet with a row of ornate lampposts on the outer side. First he lifted the bicycle up next to him, then put out his hand to help Miss Anita climb up.

She joined him without hesitation, although she had no idea what he intended to do. She watched him get on the bicycle, but didn't respond immediately when he gestured for her to sit back on the bar. She leaned over a little and looked into the murky mass of the river with the flickering reflection of streetlights on its surface.

She raised her eyes to his smiling face, gazed at it for a while, smiled finally in return and got on the bar. He was now cycling slowly, formally, as though on parade. The lampposts they passed resembled a lineup of grenadiers.

They stopped in the middle of the bridge because something was blocking their way. He got off the bike, onto the parapet, and she did the same. He picked up the bicycle, held it over his head several moments, swung it and then let it go. She clapped as it curved downwards, hit the water with a splash and disappeared into the gloomy depths.

He bent down to pick up what was lying on the parapet. First he took the raincoat and held it out for her. It was a man's, at least two sizes too big and with mismatched lapels, but this didn't bother her in the slightest.

Then he handed her the scarf. She readily placed it around her neck, even though she didn't like yellow. There were two large dark spots on one end that made it more attractive.

He dropped down on his left knee, right foot forward, slowly untied the laces of the white sneaker and took it off. Then he grabbed her right foot above the ankle, raised it a little, took off her shoe without unbuckling it and hurled it into the river.

When he had replaced her shoe with his sneaker and tied the lace, she discovered that it was neither too small nor too large. She did not find this strange. How natural, she thought, for a mother and son to have identical feet.

The shoe on her left foot ended up in the water too, but she received nothing in return. When he rose and stood next to her, they had one shoe each. The two shoes were side by side again, but the same person wasn't wearing them.

He held out his hand. She took it and he bowed his head. She did the same and saw a boat starting to appear from under the bridge. It was magnificently lit and decorated with pennants, full of cheerful music and people waving at them.

When it got about halfway out, it stopped. The young man turned towards Miss Anita and smiled once again. She returned his smile, as she had at the beginning of the bridge. There was no need to say anything.

Their bare feet stepped forward in unison. They plummeted, but there was no danger. When they reached the deck, their landing on the sneakers would be as soft as down.

AFTERWORD

THE BRIDGE BETWEEN HUMANISM AND POSTHUMANISM

SLOBODAN VLADUŠIĆ

A first reading of *The Bridge* leaves the impression of a pervasive Kafkaesque atmosphere that is hard to resist. I wonder, though, in Carver-like fashion: what do we really mean when we say Kafkaesque? There are as many enigmas of interpretation,[1] perhaps, as there are enigmas of literary origin hidden behind this ordinary attribute.[2] Its purpose seems to be to subdue the enigma of a writer and his imaginary world in which the inconceivable and the alogical can never be vanquished.

If Živković's book were just the echo of a world classic, this would be a recommendation to read it, but not necessarily interpret it. In line with the hermeneutics of questions and answers, we can ask ourselves the following: what question reappears on the contemporary reader's horizon after the realization that Kafka's answer may no longer

---

[1] See: Milivoj Solar, "Paradoxes of Interpretation" ("Paradoksi tumačenja") in *Myth of the Avant-Garde and Myth of Decadence* (*Mit o avangardi i mit o dekadenciji*), Nolit, Belgrade, 1985.

[2] See: H. I. Borges, "Kafka and His Precursors" ("Kafka i njegove preteče"), *Prose, Poetry, Essay* (*Proza, poezija, esej*), Bratstvo jedinstvo, Novi Sad, 1986.

be sufficient? In order to address this issue, we first need to answer another question: what is it that made Kafka part of the canon of world literature and of the broader cultural heritage such that his last name has become an attribute denoting a certain notion of the world?

We recall the influential study *The Fantastic: A Structural Approach to a Literary Genre* in which Tzvetan Todorov centers the fantastic on the protagonist's dilemma as to the nature of the events unfolding around him.[3] The protagonist wonders whether the events can be rationally explained or not, and it is this perplexity that enables the reader to identify with him.

In *The Trial*, such a definition of the fantastic is challenged, since Joseph K. shows no bewilderment and quickly accepts the presence of the Tribunal and the trial being conducted against him. The reader is thus unable to identify with the protagonist. At least not a reader who bases their understanding of the fantastic on the works analyzed by Tzvetan Todorov as primary examples of the fantastic. This seems to bear out Sava Damnjanov's passing remark that Todorov has a 19th century understanding of the fantastic and is thereby dated.[4] In this respect, Todorov could be read as a theoretician of so-called "traditional" fantasy.

If Joseph K. consents too hastily to the trial being conducted against him, this haste indicates that any rational alternative to the fantastic has disappeared, although one still existed in the 19th century. Kafka places the source of the irrational in social institutions as the product of human rationality which, before him, had been the tacit foundation of the protagonist's rationality as set against the (super)natural and otherworldly. When the irrational appears in a place where the rational used to reside, then the actions of Kafka's protagonists are no longer strongholds of common sense and the reader's refuge in a

---

[3] Tzvetan Todorov, *The Fantastic: A Structural Approach to a Literary Genre* (*Uvod u fantastičnu književnost*), Rad, Belgrade, 1987.

[4] Sava Damnjanov, *Roots of Modern Serbian Literature of the Fantastic* (*Koreni moderne srpske fantastike*), Matica srpska, Novi Sad, 1988, p. 35.

dubious world. That is when the protagonists become irrational too. This is shown by the examples of land surveyor K. and Joseph K., but is probably most apparent in the case of Gregor Samsa, transformed into a roach. Instead of the rational protagonist of traditional fantastic stories, the protagonist is now fantastic, and what should be an irrational threat has become a typical rational family. *The Metamorphosis*—now the symbolical depth of the title can be seen. Not only the protagonist and the fantastic story metamorphose, but also the relationship between rational and irrational: the irrational does not threaten the rational, rather the exact opposite.

Kafka's turnabout within the layout of traditional fantastic would be less striking were it not for the fact that it corresponds to the philosophical insight of a similar turnabout that happens in Enlightenment. This turnabout is perhaps most concisely expressed by Max Horkheimer and Theodor Adorno in their *Dialectic of Enlightenment*. The very first sentence of this book suggests the paradoxical "changing sides" that we note in Kafka. "In the most general sense of progressive thought, the Enlightenment has always aimed at liberating men from fear and establishing their sovereignty. Yet the fully enlightened earth radiates disaster triumphant."[5] In the light of reason, what appeared was not a liberated man but an enslaved, outdated man,[6] as he is called by Gunther Anders, not by chance one of the most important interpreters of Kafka's opus.[7] Interest in Kafka's opus developed parallel to this insight into the paradoxical nature of Enlightenment: they fueled each other.

We can just imagine that moment in the bright light of the Rational when the irrational, not folly, appeared. This was a watershed moment for humanity, because the world in which it had based the very concept of humaneness collapsed before its eyes. If words are still part of

---

[5] Max Horkheimer, Theodor Adorno, *Dialectic of Enlightenment* (*Dijalektika prosvetiteljstva*), Veselin Masleša, Svjetlost, Sarajevo, 1989, p. 17.

[6] See: Gunther Anders, *The Outdatedness of Human Beings* (*Zastarelost čoveka*), Nolit, Belgrade, 1985.

[7] See: Gunther Anders, *Kafka – pro und contra*, Narodna prosvjeta, Sarajevo, 1955.

reason because they have meaning and create meaning when spoken one after the other, then this very fact makes them anachronous and superfluous for Kafka. A man appears in *The Trial*, "made weak and thin by the height and distance, [who] leaned suddenly far out from it and stretched his arms out even further."[8] A little later, Joseph K. finds himself in the same position, and this analogy between the two men creates an ironic, unconscious communication in which there are no words. And where there are words—at the very end of *The Trial* when the almost dead Joseph K. speaks—they do not call forth other words. When Joseph K. describes his death with the ellipsis "Like a dog!" the men do not react. This very utterance reduces Joseph K. to an animal, a dog, a dehumanized victim. The exclamation mark at the end of the sentence, that raised voice, signals a yearning for the words still to be heard and for them to prevail.

The exclamation mark at the end of Kafka's *The Trial* echoes the expressionistic *scream*[9]—a sound that summons not only the absolute fear and anxiety of the modernist but also suggests distrust in language and words as forms of socialization and the foundation of human solidarity. The scream is the concentrated fear of the individual's fate,[10] which raises the question of their future after the realization that the modernist project has failed. In answer to this question, on the wings of high modernity appears the regressive figure of the individual:

---

[9] As interpreted by Bojana Stojanović Pantović, the scream, along with ectasy and an apocalyptic vision, is a manifestation of the expressionistic longing to overcome anxiety and alienation. See: Bojana Stojanović Pantović, *Expressionism* (*Ekspresionizam*), Matica srpska, Novi Sad, 1998, p. 28.

[10] We should be careful here. The scream that appears at the end of Rastko Petrović's polyvalent genre text *People Speak* (*Ljudi govore*) unites the *pre-human* and the human at the moment of birth, when life begins. In this respect, Rastko greatly differs from the expressionistic scream that represents the ultimate stage of alienation and fear. Turned at the same time towards the mystery of birth, Rastko gives evidence of modern skepticism towards the figure of man, because by betting on birth, Rastko is actually betting on some unattained modernity, some eternal future.

mythical man, or a barbarian bringing the solution, as in Kavafi's well-known verses or Micić's concept of the decivilizing *barbarogen*.

Threatening the individual, on the other hand, leads to elated non-humaneness, and it is in this context that the futuristic admiration of technology should be read that subsequently leads to elated war as a magnificent, destructive orgy of technology. This elation finds its roots in a different understanding of man, such as that found in Jinger's diaries from the First World War in which the military spirit consistently avoids any sort of humanistic conclusion before the horrors of the artillery "storm of steel", at the same time glorifying war as a special situation in which a person can find self-confirmation in a completely different way than during peacetime. Nevertheless, this new military man is still not superman, as a more modern type of individual.

It would be interesting to find out when the attribute *Kafkaesque* first appeared. I suspect it was after the Second World War as an appeasing word in which absolute modernistic fear anchored itself and petered out. This fear emerged in the wake of recent historical horror, the paradoxical nature of the Enlightenment and Kafka's equally paradoxical fantastic, both founded on the same turnabout: the transformation of the rational into the irrational and reason into non-reason. The attribute *Kafkaesque* is thus part of the process of *becoming accustomed* to the irrational appearing in places where—had the program of Enlightenment not been crushed—the rational would have had to prevail. This peaceful word—peaceful compared to the scream or summoning barbarian solutions—is somewhat imbued with an atmosphere of the postmodern cynicism described in Sloterdijk's *Critique of Cynical Reason*: "The modern cynic is said to be understood as a borderline melancholic, one who is able to keep the symptoms of depression under control and keep up appearances at both home and work."[11] The melancholy and bitterness[12] mentioned by Sloterdijk fit

---

[11] Peter Sloterdijk, *Critique of Cynical Reason* (*Kritika ciničnog uma*), Globus nakladni zavod, Zagreb, 1992, p. 21.

[12] "His actions are underscored by constant bitterness", *ibid*.

in well with the description of this atmosphere: every mention of the word *Kafkaesque* has at least an iota of lamentation for the loss of an idea, the idea of enlightenment, a loss that seems impossible to forget. Or can it be forgotten?

Sloterdijk's melancholic, bitter cynicism does not exactly agree with the postmodern euphoria evoked by one of its melancholic critics. Frederic Jameson associated this euphoria with Kant's definition of the exalted. The feeling of exaltation appears as a result of the inability of man's consciousness to conceive of the size of some architecture and so it appears as absolutely large or absolutely inconceivable. Jameson rightfully notes that the exaltation of technology no longer rests on earlier forms of technological size, such as "turbines . . . silos and chimneys, or Baroque renderings of pipelines and assembly lines, and not even in the aerodynamic profile of trains"[13] but rather on the computer. As a result, the feeling of exaltation—that mixture of awe and horror—is caused by the world-wide web, economic, social, IT; however it is denoted, it is something that man's consciousness cannot conceive. This universal networking and interconnectivity is the source of postmodern euphoria that continues, as we will see, as the equally euphoric new concept of man and humanity.

Now it is possible to show why the attribute *Kafkaesque* essentially clashes with the atmosphere of Zoran Živković's *The Bridge*, for this novel casts doubt upon a central characteristic of the fantastic world—the *threat* surrounding the protagonist.

The world of the fantastic is an interactive world insofar as it takes the role of the protagonist,[14] in some interpretations, and is thereby revealed as a threat to the protagonist. In *The Trial*, this threat is paradoxical: Joseph K. is arrested but is left in his own apartment as though

---

[13] Frederic Jameson, "Postmodernism: The Cultural Logic of Late Capitalism" ("Postmodernizam ili kulturna logika kasnog kapitalizma"), *The Postmodern (New Epoch or Misconception)* (*Postmoderna (nova epoha ili zabluda)*), Belgrade, 1984, p. 134.

[14] See: F. Jameson, "Magical Narratives" ("Magična pripovedanja"), *Politically Unaware* (*Političko nesvesno*), translated by Dušan Puhalo, Rad, Belgrade, 1984, p. 134.

nothing has happened. The reason for the Tribunal's gradual closing in on Joseph K. should be sought in the imaginary world of Kafka's novel: the totality of the interactive network in the imaginary world is more present and at the same time less visible than in the traditional fantastic in which the existence of fantastic chronotypes, such as a castle in a Gothic novel, indicates the restricted *part* of space in which the fantastic world will appear in the form of some sort of spectral (and not divine) hierophant. In Kafka, however, *everything* belongs to the Tribunal and so the Tribunal is all around the protagonist of *The Trial*, and in him as well, because he casts no doubt upon it: thus, instead of the story advancing and resolving the protagonist's/reader's perplexity regarding the nature of the events, as happens in traditional fantastic stories, here the story is about the impossibility of any such advancement within the world of the Tribunal, in spite of accepting it. The protagonist's death is not the result of some visible progress in the trial, but is as irrational as the arrest at the beginning of the novel.

Živković's *The Bridge* suggests a postmodern alternative to this modernistic Kafkaesque narrative on the impossibility of advancing in the world of the fantastic and total interconnection that dehumanizes/kills the individual. In *The Bridge*, a seemingly Kafkaesque atmosphere is transformed into postmodern euphoria that is accompanied by an awareness of the interconnectivity of the world which, for Živković, is more the possibility of a new life than a threat to life, as it is for Kafka. This semantic shift can be shown by comparing Živković's novel to Kafka's. First of all, in spite of its seemingly "non-obligatory" nature, the arrest in *The Trial* suggests the protagonist's obligation to the Tribunal, for in the imaginary world of Kafka's novel there is no stance outside of the Tribunal. Such a stance nonetheless exists in the imaginary world of Živković's novel: it is situated in the repeated *bewilderment* of Živković's protagonists. This enables the reader to identify with the protagonist.

At first glance, Živković seems to be taking one step back from Kafka and not ahead of him, as we are trying to show here. This first impression is deceptive, though. Unlike traditional fantastic that insists on perplexity with regard to the nature of the event (whether or not the event has a rational explanation), the narrators in all three chapters of Živković's novel do not resolve this dilemma, as a rule, because everything that is known in this regard is *already* known at the beginning of the chapter.

Where Kafka has coercion (the arrest), Živković has free will. And where doubt as to the nature of events appears in Tzvetan Todorov's analyses, such doubt exists in Živković as well but is *never* resolved. This *twofold difference* gives rise to an unexpected imaginary world in which the protagonists follow a double, a deceased neighbor and an unborn son, but not from the desire to wrench themselves away from some sort of coercion or find out the real nature of the person they are following.

So why are they following them?

This question is not easy to answer, perhaps because of Živković's singular style where the term minimalist is not enough. The expression "phenomenological reduction" might be used, in the metaphorical sense of course, in order to clarify the link between Živković's style and the thrust of the novel. The reader might feel Živković's writing is a radical return to the very essence of things, which means removing any symbolic meaning or intertextual link that things might attract into their orbit. At the same time, the status of the characters (a double, a dead neighbor, an unborn child) and the absurdity of their actions, seen from a realistic viewpoint of course, result in a very deep chasm between Živković's text and mimicry. If we add the actual anonymity of the narrators who are reduced to record keepers of the oddities of a world, then it becomes clear that reading Živković's prose leads the reader to the question "and then what happened?" The purpose of this question is provided by the constant *advancement* of the person being followed by the protagonist. The impression of advancing again lies in the fact that the character's actions fit together like some sort of puzzle, and they also *fit together* on a higher level of interaction between various characters. All of this indicates that behind the apparently absurd acts of the protagonists lies a structure that is slowly being perceived.[15]

Reading *The Bridge* starts to resemble the genre of video games known as *adventure*. In the imaginary world of the adventure, objects have a special meaning that is based only somewhat on real-world logic, while their *specific* importance arises within the context of the game they are in. Furthermore, this means that there is no intercultural, symbolical meaning, since video games are distributed all over the world and must not contain any specific cultural codes, unless they are pop icons. It is not hard to guess that the adventure starts with the question "and then what happened?" The answer takes the player gradually away from real-world logic towards the logic of the imaginary world of adventure. This substitution is never complete because then the player's identification with the protagonist would be jeopardized and the player-controlled protagonist would turn into a character from a film that the player could not control, since he or she could never master the rules of such an imaginary world without the mediating role of real-world logic.

The question "and then what happened?" is answered by successfully resolving the tasks/riddles which, with a bit of simplification, can be reduced to transferring an object correctly from one place to another, or from one character to another. Solving these riddles is slow going at first because the specific logic of the imaginary world of adventure is unknown, and then speeds up as the tasks are resolved more rapidly with gradual advancement of the game when this specific logic becomes clearer and more familiar to the player.

The adventure's progress does not depend on the player's reflexes, which means that scenes of violence are detached from the player either

---

[15] The fact that no progress is made in our understanding of the Tribunal in Kafka's *The Trial* is shown by polemics regarding Max Brod's ordering of the chapters. Regardless of whether or not these objections are justified, the very fact that they exist indicates the fragmentary structure of *The Trial*, which, owing to this fragmented state, removes the possibility of any progress in our understanding of the Tribunal.

by the time and place of events (the player only sees the results of the violence) or by animating part of the game where the player is unable to act. There is ideological meaning in taking violence out of the playable part of the adventure or putting it beyond the player's view: it suggests the player's absolute safety, since violence passes by without touching him or her. Even if the player-controlled protagonist in a game dies as a result of some uncompleted task, this death is only virtual: the player is not on the same ontological plane as the protagonist and numerous mechanisms (e.g. recording positions in the world of adventure) can bring the protagonist back to life. The world of adventure thus proves to be an absolutely safe world.

Equating the fantastic world of adventure with absolute safety is not without consequences, for it contains the idea of a harmless fantastic that over time turns into a welcoming and desirable fantastic. Traditional fantastic sees the irrational as a threat to the rational and Kafka's fantastic turns rational into threatening irrational. Živković's *The Bridge*, however, is closer to an understanding of the fantastic in which rationality and humanity become the threat: rationality threatens because it brings cognizance of death and humanity again becomes a synonym for mortal man, a being that cannot resist death. Rescue lies not in the hands of reason or some super-rational solidarity such as might be suggested by the ending of *The Trial*, but in a fantastic that has the form of something *about to be real*.

"Rescue" fantastic appears today in the form of posthumanism that goes beyond humanistic limitations, the first and foremost being man's short life. In these posthumanist reveries, the fantastic goes from science fiction to fiction science. This hiatal transformation condenses the difference between science fiction and fiction science into a period of time known as "just about". The posthumanist atmosphere of serenity and optimism is nominally based on science, while its actual roots are in faith in its speed. Here is a symptomatic excerpt from a transhumanist blog that illustrates posthumanist enthusiasm quite well:

"Do you want to live 50,000 years or more? Do you want to be able to build a house from the foundation up, have an IQ of 500, get rid of unwanted character traits and memories? In the not-so-distant future you will be able to do all these things and many, many more."[16]

It's no accident that the list of posthumanist improvements starts with a longer life. The posthumanist idea could thus be defined as a leap from human qualities to eternal life, which inevitably includes the need to die like a man. Since this death is now conceived as passing to the almost eternal life offered by fiction science, it's no accident that this death must happen in a humanistic milieu but without humanistic consequences.

The ultimate merit of Živković's *The Bridge* is how strikingly it evokes this last act of humanity and first act of posthumanism. This can be seen in the central motif of the bridge. A humanistic "reading" of the bridge motif is not at issue, particularly not in Serbian literature where such an interpretation appears in important works by its great writer Ivo Andrić, not only the novel *Bridge on the Drina* or one of Andrić's best stories *Bridge on the Žepa*, but also the essay entitled *Bridges* in which such a humanistic reading of bridges is clearly stated.

Andrić found that bridges "belong to everyone and are equally useful to one and all, always built by design."[17] It is not hard to see universal humanistic values in this praise of bridges: equality, usefulness, purpose. In order for the bridge to retain these characteristics, however, it had to be conceived as a form bridging specific obstacles, that later, in humanistic discourse, became a predictable metaphor. Andrić: "All around the world, wherever my thoughts wander or settle, they come across faithful and silent bridges like the eternal human desire, eternally insatiable, to link, reconcile and connect everything that appears before our body and soul, lest there be divisions, opposition and partings."[18]

---

[16] http://transhumanist.blogspot.com/

[17] Ivo Andrić, "Bridges" ("Mostovi") in *Paths, People, Landscapes* (*Staza, lica, predela*), Collected Works Vol. 10, Prosveta, Mladost, Svjetlost, Državna založba Slovenije, Belgrade-Zagreb-Sarajevo-Ljubljana, 1963, p. 199.

[18] *Ibid*, p. 201.

It is not too difficult to note that Andrić anticipates some other types of bridges here, such as bridgeheads as a military interpretation of the desire for universal integration. Even such a military reading of bridges still sees them in a humanistic form advancing to the other bank.

Andrić provides for another important symbolical potential of the bridge that must remain obscure because it is turned towards death, not progress. This is the bridge visited by suicides. The collective quality of bridges, emphasized by Andrić in the title of his essay ("Bridges" and not "Bridge"!) and the narration on different types and shapes of bridges, on their collective use and collective usefulness, dissipates in the jump of the lonely suicide, since this jump, this perspective of the bridge, clearly points to the hopeless separation of the individual from the collective.

Just as a humanistic reading of the bridge must exclude the lonely, suicidal jump off the bridge in order to retain its pathos, the jump of two people instead of one—suicides—is unimaginable for such a "suicidal" reading of the bridge. If the subterranean thought that orchestrates the suicide is actually the desire to make a distinction between oneself and society, then a double suicide is a farce. For this reason, the jump of two protagonists at the end of Živković's novel deviates from both the humanistic and the suicidal treatment of the bridge. Unlike the humanistic reading, for Živković hope no longer lies on the other bank, i.e. in the eternal advancement of the humanistic idea that bridges over all obstacles, but in a jump into the unknown. From the humanistic perspective, it is impossible to know where the protagonists will land after they jump! Contrary to the lonely, suicidal reading turned towards death, Živković's protagonists jump together. Where a suicidal view sees the water awaiting them, the posthumanist view sees a boat where the jumpers will be greeted by merriment—the symbol of postmodern euphoria and posthumanist cheerfulness.

Now, of course, other questions arise: if the humanistic bridge leads to the other bank, where is the posthumanist boat headed? And what kind of a boat is it, anyway? A ferryboat of the dead like Charon's? A boat full of folly like Brant's *Narrensciff*? Or is it a new, posthumanist Argo?

Our children will know the answer.

THE BRIDGE

What is the link between red hair, a red bowling ball and a red bikini? Between an overcoat with asymmetrical lapels, a scarf with two blotches and a pair of non-matching sneakers? In this brainteasing trio of stories, Zoran Živković explores the collision of realities: a man encounters an alternate self, a woman out on a shopping trip runs into her dead neighbour and a fourteen-year-old girl chases her seventeen-year-old future son across town. Through absurd predicament, surreal situations and hot pursuit, Živković addresses deep and ultimately poignant questions of fate and chance, the vagaries of human character and the hidden potential which lies within us all.

ABOUT THE AUTHOR

Zoran Živković was born in Belgrade, former Yugoslavia, in 1948. He graduated from the Department of General Literature with the theory of literature, Faculty of Philology of the University of Belgrade; he later received his master's and doctorate degrees from the same school.

He is the author of *The Fourth Circle, The Writer, The Book, Impossible Stories, Hidden Camera, Compartments, Four Stories Till the End, The Reader, Twelve Collections & The Teashop, Amarcord, The Last Book,* and *Escher's Loops.*

He lives in Belgrade, Serbia, with his wife Mia, their sons Uroš and Andreja, and their four cats.